EFFIE'S HOUSE

Effie's
House

by Morse
Hamilton

Greenwillow Books
N E W   Y O R K

Printed in the United States of America
First Edition   1 2 3 4 5 6 7 8 9 10

Library of Congress Cataloging-in-Publication Data
Hamilton, Morse.
Effie's House/by Morse Hamilton.
p.   cm.
Summary: A teenage girl with a terrible secret runs
away from home, seeking counsel from the father
she will not believe was killed in Vietnam.
ISBN 0-688-09307-8
[1. Emotional problems—Fiction.
2. Runaways—Fiction.   3. Pregnancy—Fiction.
4. Fathers and daughters—Fiction.
5. Mothers and daughters—Fiction.
6. Vietnamese Conflict, 1961–1975—Fiction.]
I. Title.   PZ7.H18265Ef 1990
[Fic]—dc20   89-11918   CIP   AC

ACKNOWLEDGMENTS

We gratefully acknowledge the following permissions:

The quotation on page 145 is from "Hey Jude" by John Lennon and Paul McCartney, © 1968 NORTHERN SONGS LTD. All Rights for the U.S., Canada and Mexico Controlled and Administered by SBK BLACKWOOD MUSIC INC. Under License from ATV MUSIC (MACLEN). All Rights Reserved. International Copyright Secured. Used by Permission.

The line "I learn by going where I have to go" on page 192 is from "The Waking" by Theodore Roethke, copyright © 1948 by Theodore Roethke, which appeared in THE COLLECTED POEMS OF THEODORE ROETHKE, published by DOUBLEDAY, a division of Bantam, Doubleday, Dell Publishing Group, Inc. Reprinted by permission of the publisher.

TO
SHARON
EMILY
KATE
&
ABIGAIL

Some also have wished that the next way to their father's house were here, and that they might be troubled no more with either hills or mountains to go over, but the way is the way, and there is an end.

—JOHN BUNYAN

EFFIE'S HOUSE

Clare County Hospital, somewhere in the state of Michigan, September 2. Nice new notebook with one hundred fifty 8½-×-11-inch, college-ruled sheets, a gift of Father Jude, the Catholic clergyman or whatever you call him. I'm trying to get used to the fact that it has a snot green cover. He looked so adorable, taking his hands out of his pockets to explain it was all they had in the shop downstairs. I gave him the thumbs-up for thank you.

Notes for the incredible story I might tell the good father if he visits me again—though then again I might not, I might not tell him anything.

By the way, if anyone finds this notebook and reads it without my permission, I hope your gonads dry up or fall off, as the case may be. Beware.

—*E. B.*

H
ow
I los
t my fa
ther& & &
& & & & & &
& & &   & & &

&

I picture him slouching in the front seat of his car, with just his eyes peering out, while all around him the parking lot is gathering dark, and across the river the slow-moving stream of headlights quietly leaves the city. I wasn't there, but I can imagine how it was: Just as he shows up, everyone else has left or is leaving, but he comes on anyway, having the inbound lanes pretty much to himself. Kind of amazed to be getting there at all, after all these years, pounding on the steering wheel lightly in his excitement.

I have no trouble imagining how he would have felt: This was indubitably the correct, the most excellent moment to be arriving in our nation's capital! You would want to get to Ho Chi Minh City on a rainy August afternoon with pajama-clad bicyclists whispering past on their way to destinations secret and inscrutable. And you would definitely want to fly into JFK long after night has fallen and the city's a heap of jewels down there. But our nation's capital looks best in the brief hour between afternoon and night, when the wide southern sky is kind of a neon blue and the old pointy-topped lights along Pennsylvania Avenue are just starting to come on, and you notice that the lights are on in the windows of all the stores in Georgetown, and the stately monuments to our nation's dead are glimmering out on the Potomac.

I hope I don't get in trouble with God for having thoughts like these. In my dreams I always hear the angry *tuck, tuck, tuck* of the chopper with its wicked tail, as it swings sideways up the river, looking for one of its own, man escaped from Fort Death, AWOL from the Hereafter. While farther to the north and west, giant headlights strafe the dark. Large lights, looming larger—*whoosh!* The plane is gone.

The bridges are almost empty now. The last cars hurry across. On the other side of the river another row of lights blinks on, each lamp shining in its own bright haze. Someone starts his engine, for it is night, Father, and time.

& &

A person, whose name I don't want to tell you yet, stops a couple of doors shy of a red-brick house in one of the Virginia suburbs of Washington, D.C. The instant his motor is switched off, like he's changed the channel or something, the noise of crickets possesses the world. Some nosy neighbor, flattening his fat, ugly nose against the window, sees the parked car, nothing more. Figures they're having another party down the block and goes back to his baseball game.

What he doesn't see is the shadow of a man slowly lean across the front seat, his eyes still on the house two doors down, or, reaching into a paper sack on the floor of the passenger side, get out the mask he bought, or, with trembling hands and sitting sideways in a sort of heap, pull the thing on over his head. Now his world smells like the inside of a bathing cap. The poor guy is breathing his own bad breath. But is he grossed out? I don't think so, because as soon as he puts it on, he's liberated himself from the need to lie low. I don't know if I'm saying this right. He feels safe for a change.

Sitting up, he tries to see himself in the rearview mirror, and when he has managed to twist the reflection of his obscene joke into view, he emits a noise that isn't laughter—that isn't anything like laughter, come to think of it. And his neck, with the muscles all tensed up like a drawing in an anatomy book, is dripping with drool.

He closes the door behind him as quietly as he can and helps himself around a chinaberry tree to the sidewalk. Scuffing along in the shadows that anxious porch lights throw over shrubs and wooden fences, he is drawing closer to the red-brick house. The crickets are humming like crazy.

Did you know, Father Jude, that in the hills above Da Nang they have a species of grasshopper that sounds exactly like a telephone ringing? Can you imagine the sound a million of them make?

Tall, dark shadow of a man scuffing along, crickets screaming, phones ringing. He pauses in front of the red-brick house, stares at the number over the door to make sure, steals up the driveway. *Thup!* He stops, folds his arms over his chest, looks around wildly.

That's only Eric's Wiffle Ball you stepped on, Mr. Shadow Man. Outraged, it scoots onto the Hertigs' lawn, glares whitely in the grass. At the middle window the Thin Man stops. Putting both hands on the brick sill, he gets up on his tiptoes and peers in. It's dark inside, except for the one light we always leave on in the front hall, supposedly to scare burglars away, and maybe another one in the TV room that I forgot to turn off, though it's definitely not television light shining on his mask.

He stands there, peering in—actually, peeping is more like it, since only his eyes are above the sill. But there's no one inside to see them, except for Anya, the cat, who's probably asleep on the couch as usual. But maybe he sees someone we can't see. Maybe he sees Hattie Topham Bridges Curtis Karpathy Comstock soon-to-be Smith, the world-famous documentary video maker. Sees her as she looked sixteen years ago, before she'd acquired the last four names, sitting in her corner of the sofa, reading one of her psychobabble books by the light of a single lamp, her legs tucked under her, Anya perched on her lap, sitting in her own little tent, as she turns the page, chancing to look up at the window and catching sight of—*Who is that out there‽‽*

In other words, my mom, the light of my life, the bane of my life.

I have a whole box of pictures from when she was younger, because no one in our family even bothers to put them in albums, and, boy, was she pretty back then with long brown hair, a wicked smile, a look that said this woman's not afraid of any camera—or cameraman.

In the one I used to keep by my bed, she is sitting in a boat somewhere here in Michigan, in a granny dress that cannot hide how—ahem—pregnant she is (for a certain person had already left heaven and was on her way to the Valley of the Living). Her long hair is tied in a psychedelic neckerchief like Pocahontas. There are flowers painted on her cheeks. The way her mouth is open, the way her arms are crossed, the way she's staring straight at the camera, it looks like she's just said something gross and is kind of pleased with herself.

When I get older, I plan to be like that.

You can't see my dad because—duh—he's the one taking the picture. They were both very young at the time; my dad was just a teenager.

> She sits back against the bow,
> Looks at him, amused—
> I know that look and
> How he must have felt,
> Spying on her through the aperture
> On a day of light and shadow—
> The brim of her hat eclipses her brow.
> She is merry without smiling, he hopes.
> I hope.
> This is long before I was born.

I thought that was a pretty good beginning to a not-bad poem when I wrote it for Ms. Plover's English class last year, but nobody I showed it to seemed to understand what it was supposed to be about. The "aperture" of a, you know, camera. "Bow" as in boat. It's a photograph of my mom on her honeymoon, okay, wit-nit?

Not that she looks that way anymore, despite all the Jane Fonda exercises she does in front of the VCR. But she isn't bad for a woman her age.

Anyway, she's not home.

The mystery man's been standing like that for going on five minutes, peeping in at the window, and I'm getting the fidgets. Up until now he's followed my directions to the letter, almost like I'm the one who's been drawing his car through the darkening streets by remote control or something. And just when he's almost here, and I'm impatient to be off, he has to stop and window-peek. Doesn't he know how hard this is for me? Doesn't he understand that *I'm burning my bridges*—ha ha—behind me?

In my mind I say, Keep coming, mister. Just a few more steps, and Mr. Hertig won't be able to see you from his kitchen window where he's always washing dishes. And then I can show myself.

At last, slowly, he lifts his hand—not Mr. Hertig, the man who's looking in our window. He lifts his hand like he's going to wave at someone, only uses it instead to chase away a bug, or a vision. And when he finally pulls away from the side of the house, I see that he's kind of aged, too, which makes sense, since in reality he'd only be a couple of years younger than my mom.

If you want to know the truth, he looks like all the life has been bled out of him—sort of the way I always imagined Bone looks in the game my future stepsister, Kate, is always playing. You know, you flatten your face with your hands and chant in a hillbilly accent, "Hi, my name is

Bone. My daddy calls me Bone, my mama calls me Bone, my sister calls me Bone, my brother calls me Bone, and my dog calls me Bone. One day my mama said, 'Bone, how can you frown through all that bone?' and I said, 'Look!'"

By tugging up on his rubber chin, the intruder lifts the bottom of his mask away from his face, and you can see from the rising and falling of his narrow shoulders that he's trying to catch his breath. I can hear him sort of growling, too. He wipes his neck and the front of his jacket with a handkerchief, then holds it, wadded up, over his heart, like he's saying the Pledge of Allegiance. Finally he puts the handkerchief away, adjusts the mask, and looks around the backyard.

Now that I can see the mask he's wearing, I don't know whether to laugh or what. It's one of those Richard Nixon masks you see in joke shops. You know, Richard Nixon, as in Vietnam and Watergate.

I can't stand still another second. I cough. I go to take a giant step out of the garage, only it turns out to be more like an umbrella step.

I start to whisper something stupid like "Is that you?" but unfortunately it comes out as "What took you so long?"

He doesn't move a muscle.

I walk all the way out to where he can see me in the light from the stars and the neighbors' windows. I put my hand up and say, "Hi."

The poor guy. In slow motion, without making a sound, he brings both hands together and makes a deep obeisance, like the former President on his trip to China (which we saw a film about in school).

"Can you nod or something for yes?"

11

He nods.

"That's good. I have to do all the talking, right? Mom says I'd rather talk than eat, which isn't exactly true, as you can see. Ready to go? I am. My stuff's in there."

We get my stuff, which is piled on top of the garbage can. Then I mumble, "Oh, I guess I'm forgetting something," and put my guitar case down. I make myself go up to him. He's wearing a frayed pilot's jacket. His chest is warm. He smells like medicine. "Welcome home, Daddy." I don't know how hard it's safe to hug him.

A few seconds later we've sneaked through the Hertigs' yard, around to where his car is parked. We're gone.

Dear Father Jude,

I'll tell you anything you want to know *in writing*, but I've taken a vow of silence and don't wish ever to speak again. I especially don't have anything to say to the police or the headshrinkers. I respect you as someone the Lord has called, though I'm not 100-percent positive I believe in the Lord, and I'm thinking of becoming a Catholic, although I have to warn you that I'm very much in favor of birth control and I'm not what you'd call a Pro-Lifer. I personally could never get an abortion, but I believe women should be able to decide for themselves. Would that disqualify me?

Also, while I'm thinking of it, could you please say something to the dietitian about not bringing me meat? I don't believe in eating my fellow creatures, so it just goes to waste.

Thank you for coming to see me and for saying you would be willing to listen to anything I have to say. I appreciate your concern.

You asked if I had any of my dad's letters. I'm afraid not. He told me to destroy them, which I did. I tore them up and flushed them down the toilet. I wish now I'd saved at least one, especially the first one, which I'll tell you about.

In 1968 my real father (because I have about a hundred stepfathers), Richard Bridges, was listed as Missing in Action, and the following year Missing was changed to Killed, don't ask me why. All anyone knows for sure is that a search-and-rescue patrol he was on got ambushed and there were some casualties. One of his buddies reported that Private First Class Bridges suffered a quote unquote facial wound. But nobody actually *saw* him get killed.

I was only a baby at the time, but I know for a fact that the anxiety, first of not knowing and then of finding out that he was presumed dead, nearly killed my mom. Her milk dried up and she couldn't nurse me anymore, so unfortunately I was a bottle-fed baby, which, according to one of my headshrinkers, explains everything.

Anyway, my mom loved my dad more than any of her other husbands—of which she has had not a few—and everyone who knew him says he was special, which I believe, too. In the movie my grandma has of their wedding,

13

which took place in the woods outside of Detroit, he looks a little like James Dean, the movie star—though my mom says the only things they had in common were their sudden mood swings and the fact that their ears stuck out. When I was a little kid, I used to write him letters and bury them in the backyard.

So what does any of this have to do with the man in the Nixon mask? You know how congressmen are always going over to Vietnam with lists of names? Like what if they discovered my dad wasn't dead after all—HE WAS ALIVE!!! That he'd been living all these years in the hills above Da Nang with an old peasant couple, working in the rice paddies, and—though it's none of my business—that he had a Vietnamese girlfriend or common-law wife, maybe even some Amerasian kids?

I wouldn't mind having a stepmother, for a change, and wouldn't it be something if I had some little Vietnamese half brothers and sisters? Little Melissa Gilberts with slanted and serious-looking eyes—because everyone says I look like Melissa Gilbert on "Little House on the Prairie."

That he was badly shot up and almost unrecognizable, but alive. And the authorities in Hanoi said, "We thought he was a Cambodian. Honest mistake. Take him." So the congressmen pinned a medal on his pajamas and flew him back to an army hospital outside Valley Forge, Pennsylvania. The only problem was that he wouldn't say anything. He just lay in bed all day, playing dumb, while the plastic surgeons tried to do something with his face. But at night, when no one else was around, say he wrote to me.

I don't know how he tracked me down. The first letter— I opened it, figuring it was from my friend Jenny in New Hampshire, only it said, "Please read this in private and

14

don't say anything to anybody about it, especially not to your mom." What is this, some kind of joke? I thought. But to be on the safe side, I went up to my room and locked the door. I didn't know what was going on. Maybe I had a secret boyfriend I didn't know about???

The letter was about six pages long and written on both sides. It began by saying there was a possibility that my dad was still alive, and then after a while he said *he* was my dad and the only thing he wanted was to see his daughter, me, once before he died. He said I should write back, but not as his daughter. I was supposed to pretend I had gotten his name from my civics teacher, you know, and just wanted to cheer up a wounded vet.

So I wrote him back this masterpiece of fiction, telling him all about myself, the way you do in those letters, saying I sure would like to meet him someday, if he ever got better, which I hoped he would, soon. I also sent him the one good photograph I have of myself, or rather the only one that isn't pukacious.

Eventually, after we had been writing back and forth for about a month, he called me one night. He had said he might. He had given me a day and time, only it depended, he said, on whether a certain nurse was on duty or not. So I imagine he must have been in a hospital sort of like this one I'm in now.

He also explained that because of something he had to wear on his face he wouldn't be able to talk, but he could tap three times so I would know it was him. And I could talk.

So on a certain Wednesday night not long after we moved to northern Virginia I was sitting in the—ahem—master bedroom, pretending to be reading a book, but really I was watching the clock and taking my pulse every couple of minutes. Right at eight the phone rang, and I had it before it could finish ringing once.

"Hello!" I said in a louder voice than I'd meant to because it sounded like we had a bad connection. There was nothing on the other end except for sort of long-distance breathing and then, *tap, tap, tap,* like he was hitting the mouthpiece with a pen or something.

I shouted, "I've got it!"

My mother, the genius, picks up the extension downstairs. "Hello?"

"I've got it, Mom. It's for me."

She goes, "You have it, precious?"

After I heard the extension go *click,* I said, "Dad? It's okay. She hung up. It's me, Effie. Are you still there?"

A few seconds went by, then more quietly than before, *tap, tap, tap.* He must have been scared shitless when my mother, who used to be his wife, answered the phone.

"Can you hold the line a sec?" I said, and half a minute later, "Can you still hear me? I'm in the closet."

I heard him breathe. It sounded like he was laughing without a voice, if you can imagine that.

So I said, "Can I ask you something? We have to plan, okay?"

I heard him breathing again, which I figured must mean, Go ahead, ask.

"I have an idea, if you—you do want to see me, don't you?"

He spoke then for the first and only time. He said, "Uuh huunh," like someone having a hard time going to the bathroom, if you'll forgive my crudeness. I knew this meant uh huh, i.e., yes.

16

"You want me to come there? I could. I've hitchhiked before. I'm not afraid. Don't worry—nothing bad happened."

He didn't like this idea at all; I was afraid he wouldn't. He started moaning—then I heard the door open on his end, and there was a scuffling sound. Somebody said, "Everything all right in here?" It was a long time before the phone came back out from wherever he was hiding it and I could hear breathing again.

"Dad? I have to see you. You're my only hope. I can't stand it here anymore. I want to be with you."

Long silence. I felt like crying, but luckily I didn't.

"Could you come here and get me?"

This time he made a noise like somebody about to spit, which I interpreted to mean, Yes, if you want me to.

All of a sudden I was happier than I've ever been in my whole life. "You will?" I said, laughing.

And he made the noise again. I wonder what kind of expression he had on his face.

"Listen, my mom and her future husband I told you about are going to Baltimore for—gag—couple counseling at the end of August. I'm supposed to stay with my friend Stacey, but she's cool. She'll cover for me, even if I don't explain the whole thing. She can't stand this place, either."

I gave him the details. They'd be away for the whole weekend. My soon-to-be stepsister was going to stay at her grandmother's. After eight on Friday there wouldn't be anyone home for sure.

He didn't make a sound as I explained all this, so I couldn't be sure that he approved, and finally it occurred to me to ask him to tap three times if he liked the idea—if it would be okay and everything for him.

Right away he tapped three times.

"I don't want to get you into trouble," I said.

Again three taps.

"I'll be in the backyard. If I stand in the street, some of our nosy neighbors might see me and tell Stacey's mom, who'll tell my mom. Okay? Eight o'clock?"

Tap, tap, tap.

"I've been waiting all my life to meet you," I said, and he tapped about sixty times, like he'd gone berserk, only I know it meant, Same here, kiddo.

I went downstairs, where my next-in-line stepfather was sitting at his desk, wearing his unifocals or whatever you call them, going over the real estate ads in the paper. He smiled at me briefly and absentmindedly; I smiled the same way back.

My mom was in the kitchen, listening to 60s rock and roll on the radio as she washed the dishes. "Who was it, precious?" she asked as nonchalantly as she could. I knew she was dying to know. I lied and said it was this boy at the pool named Harvey Whittaker, asking me out, and she got all excited because she thinks I'm retarded socially. She thinks I'm not interested in boys. A couple of days later I told her Harvey had broken his neck or something.

&
&&&

So, a man wearing a Nixon mask, who said he was my
father, drove. And I slumped in my corner of the front seat,
my knees braced against the dash, and told him about my
myriad stepdads, who have all been hemorrhoids to live
with, except for the last one, Barry Comstock, who teaches
English at a boarding school in New England, which is a
bedpan job, if you ask me, all these spoiled rich girls
knocking on your door anytime, day or night, but he has a
weakness for spoiled rich girls—he likes it when they
knock. I told him about the little town, which of all the
places we've lived is my favorite and the one I still think
of as home, especially compared to the suburb where we
live now—you can't say town because it isn't really a
town, just a series of shopping centers in northern Virginia, where you have to drive everywhere in the car, even
to the public library, which is in a shopping center, natch,
whereas in my old town I had friends and we could walk
everywhere on real, honest-to-God sidewalks, downtown,
for example, which included a town hall and a soda shop.
And how I'd known all along Barry was bi and assumed
my mom knew, too—that and all the other stuff—and
that she was sort of resting up between heteros, but apparently she didn't and she wasn't. And, anyway, how my
next dad, quote unquote S. Leicester (Les) Smith, easily the
best-looking in the lineup—Mom has to reassure herself

she can still attract a guy like Les, which is how come we're living in the upstairs part of his split-level colonial— is the biggest jerk of all, because with all the others you could have it out and come to some kind of understanding, but Les keeps trying to take charge of my life. It's not that he's stupid, it's just that a whole part of his intelligence is missing: He has the imagination of an I-don't-know-what—I started to say a high school principal, but he's a divorce lawyer, which is how my mom met him. And he loves to strut around, tugging up on the top of his pants and saying stuff like, Now your mother and I had to make a decision here, in that voice men use when they're not sure of their authority or they're afraid you'll spot the gaping hole in their logic, which means they'll have to go back to the drawing board and come up with a new decision—I'm an authority on men, believe me. And how when he was my age *he* went to Exeter and never gets tired of mentioning the fact, since Exeter is over two hundred years old, whereas Steerforth Academy, where Barry teaches and where I did my ninth and tenth grades, is not even fifty years old and not worth mentioning in the same breath. I think going to Exeter must have been the high point of S. Leicester's life, since it's just about all he ever talks about. And he spoils his daughter, Kate, something awful, always believing her lies and taking her to Chuck E. Cheese. And somewhere in Ohio, I think it was, I conked out, and in my dream I was supposed to be taking care of this baby, only for some reason we were keeping it in one of those Styrofoam containers that Big Macs come in—I remember this worried me and I kept opening it to make sure it was still breathing in there—and in the background my soon-to-be stepsister, Kate, kept chanting, Mama had a baby and its head popped off—you know, what you say when you hold a dandelion by its stem and at the right moment flick the flower part off with your thumb. And I woke up just as we were getting off the interstate and going up the exit ramp. I smiled and stretched my arms over my head. It was still dark out, only you could tell the darkness was fading, and out the back window I saw a faint pink line.

My dad was still wearing his Nixon mask, and I was still sitting there beside him, and we were going at least a hundred miles an hour, or ninety. Or at least somewhere over the speed limit. One of the things you ought to know about me is that nothing I ever say is a complete lie, but as my mom would say, I have a tendency to *fabricate,* which is an SAT word for "make up stuff." We were going fast, which was exactly what I wanted.

Have I said anything about his car? It was an old Chevrolet, baby blue, from I think the early 50s, in mint condition, as if someone had been taking care of it for him. The windshield was much narrower than on a modern car, and it had a sort of divider in the middle, which made it look like we were a couple of gangsters in an old movie. The chrome speaker of the radio was, as far as I'm concerned, a work of art.

We stopped at a Shell station on a hill, all lit up, and I said I'd fill 'er up, which my mom lets me do all the time. He waited in the car until I got back in. Then we circled back onto the interstate. After a while he touched my shoulder and pointed to a sign that said WELCOME TO MICHIGAN, THE WATER WONDERLAND, and I smiled at him because, as he must have know, Michigan is where I was born, though I've never actually lived there, and it's where he and my mom met. I had sort of guessed that's where we were going.

I yawned. I asked what time it was. He showed me his watch.

"Almost seven," I said. "Aren't you tired?"

He shook his head.

"Can you breathe all right in that?" I asked.

He shrugged.

"Because you're going to have to take it off to eat, aren't you? If you don't mind my saying so, you look really silly driving around in a Nixon mask. I'd rather see your real face, honest."

He stared at the road ahead.

At some point I wanted to tell him about all the stuff that's been happening at home and ask his advice, but for some reason it's always harder for me to talk about anything serious in the morning. So instead I told him we had studied Nixon in school and that our history teacher said he wasn't as bad as everyone says. Vietnam and Watergate sound pretty bad to me, but I admit I don't know that much about it. I'm much better at English than I am at history or politics, and I'd rather we didn't even talk about math. My math teachers thinks I'm a cretin, but luckily my English teacher thinks I'm a genius. She says she wouldn't be surprised if I published my first novel before I go to college. I told my dad all this, stressing the good parts, and every once in a while he nodded like he was listening very carefully. Finally I said, "Are you getting hungry? Because I'm starved."

We got off at the next exit and stopped at the first likely looking place. I told him he should go in like that, with the mask on—it would cause quite a stir!

He held on to the steering wheel as if he were still driving and just stared straight ahead. I was afraid maybe I had offended him. I couldn't tell what he thought of my attempts at humor, but then I never know what people think of me.

"You wait here, okay? I'll go get our breakfast. What do you want? Bacon? Eggs? Orange juice? Coffee? Pancakes?" He kept nodding his head up and down. "Hash browns? English muffins?"

Those are all the things Barry, my other dad, used to like for breakfast.

"Don't worry," I said. "I brought money."

While I was waiting for the food, I had this urge to go over to the window and look out. And at first I thought he had disappeared because the parking lot was full of pickup trucks—nothing resembling a blue Chevy from the 50s. I can't tell you how I felt. I felt like I was falling through the floor. But then I looked again, and he was right where I had left him, his car parked under the greenwillow tree, leaning his head against the steering wheel.

Don't do that! I mouthed through the window.

I went to the ladies' room and brushed my hair and tried to imagine what it would feel like to come back after all these years, like Rip Van Winkle. I wondered what he thought of everything, like the new style of cars, and especially if I was what he had expected.

I wished I could tell what I looked like to someone who had never seen me before, but in the mirror I just looked the same as always—except, of course, bigger in the middle.

When breakfast was ready, I carried it out in a pizza box, almost spilling the orange juice, and tapped on the window with my pinky. He quickly rolled it down.

"Here you go, Tricky Dick. That'll be ten dollars—no, I'm just kidding! I already paid."

Another thing about my jokes—half the time I don't know myself what I'm going to say, which means I have to laugh at my own jokes, so people will know they're jokes and I'm not serious, which can be embarrassing. But my dad wiggled his rubber nose at me, so I guess he understood it was just a joke—the part about Tricky Dick. But I mean, it gets to you after a while to keep seeing Richard Nixon's face every time you turn around. I wonder how Julie Eisenhower stands it, ha ha.

I got back in on my side and told him it was all for him, except for one of the orange juices and the Danish, which I started eating. "I'm trying to lose weight," I explained, and then I started laughing so hard a piece of Danish popped out of my mouth, and I could have died, only this time I *was* being serious because usually I have three or four Danishes and I could easily eat ten, so just one is like going on a starvation diet.

Without looking at him I said, "You're going to have to take that off so you can eat."

Because he was just sitting there, holding a strip of bacon.

I went on nibbling my breakfast and sipping orange juice, pretending not to be watching, and finally after taking a deep breath he pulled the mask off, and I had to quickly roll down my window because I started to feel sick. But I didn't want him to know, so I started bouncing around on the seat, humming to myself and licking frosting off my finger, like nothing was the matter, only I was afraid I was going to throw up.

He looked a million times worse than I had expected.

You're going to think I'm a heartless shit, but I have to be honest. It wasn't what I expected at all, like that his face would be disfigured with awful scars or something.

He didn't have a face.

I mean, the top of his head was normal, he had hair and everything—a lot for a man his age. And his eyes—he was looking at me—were very sad, like Jesus's. But everything below the eyes was missing, except for his ears, if you count ears as part of your face, which stuck out like my mom said. The rest was just stretched skin with holes in it so he could breathe and a plastic contraption underneath to eat with. He worked it by bowing against his collarbone, which made it go *click, click, click,* and then to swallow he tilted his whole head back. He managed everything with incredible skill: He'd obviously had lots of practice. Afterwards he told me that when he first arrived at the army hospital, before he was fitted with his prosthetic jaw, all he could eat was liquids and mushed-up food. Actually, I already know about stuff like this from an article I read in a back issue of *Life* magazine.

To be honest, it looked like under the one mask he was wearing another one. It was especially hard to look at his nose holes because I kept thinking there was something even more horrible inside. You could sort of see something.

"You're not that bad," I said. "You're not a monster or anything." But then, like a baby, I started to cry. The tears plinked on my hands. I couldn't help it. I was crying for everything I realized now he had been through.

&
& &
& &

My dad didn't have to wear the Nixon mask anymore, so of course I did. And I probably would have caused an accident on the interstate if he hadn't put his hand on my shoulder and made me pull my head back in.

"Now I want to be perfectly clear," I said in a deep voice, wagging my head up and down.

You know, I've never actually seen Nixon do that, but it's what they always do on television. That, and make the V-is-for-victory sign. Which is pretty easy. I can also do a Kennedy—a Teddy Kennedy—which is a lot harder: You have to pretend you're a fat baby who's gotten into your dad's liquor cabinet.

But my specialty is my mom, not that she's really famous, except in documentary video circles, but people who know her say I'm almost as good as she is. What you do is rub your neck and stretch, because she has this thing about walking tall. And put on a brave smile, no matter what disaster has befallen you.

Anyway, I put on this show for my dad, who I was getting used to without the mask—all you had to do was concentrate on his big blue eyes. Then I got up my nerve and did an impersonation of *him*—based, I beg to remind you, ladies and gentlemen, on about eight hours' acquaintance—which consisted of throwing my head back, like some people do when they laugh, only of course not making any sound, which tickled him so much we drove across the shoulder and partway up the grass slope.

By now it was day out and warm. Around nine or so we pulled in past a sign that said HIDDEN CREEK STATE PARK. I guess because it was late in the season the place was practically deserted. The only other campers were skinheads, four guys and a girl, sitting on a picnic table, sharing a bottle and staring at us without smiling as we passed.

We drove around twice and finally picked the campsite farthest from them and the ranger's cabin. It was back in the woods, by the creek, so naturally the first thing I had to do was take my shoes and socks off and go wading, only the water turned out to be f-freezing.

All my life I've lived in towns and suburbs—my mom isn't what you'd call an outdoorsy person—and the only other time I've been camping was a weekend trip to the White Mountains with my friend Jenny and her family. So I wasn't much help putting the tent up. My dad, who was wearing a cowboy hat and a plaid neckerchief, ran around trying to raise the corners while I sat on the ground knocking in the stakes with the back of an ax. After about half an hour we got it to stay up, and then he crawled inside to take a nap while I sat in the sun and started one of the books they read at the school I might go to. I brought it along just in case I have to got back home.

In the afternoon, when my dad got up, we sat on the bank and he showed me some stuff he had written for me in his memorandum book. He had a boy's handwriting, all slanted to one side, which made me smile and look up at him. His letters to my mom all look the same way. It was stuff about him and my mom and the war. He lay on his back, and I read him this letter of his I have, out loud.

Then, before the sun went down, we drove to a nearby town and bought enough provisions to last a couple of days. When I came back out of the store, there were some people staring at the car. They didn't say anything, but you could tell what they were thinking: that my dad's blue Chevy was prettier than any car on the road today.

Needless to say, he was crouched down by the brake pedal.

Nobody else showed up at the campground, except the ranger who came by in a truck shortly after dark and said, You by yourself? I told him my dad was out collecting firewood. Can't have a fire, he said, getting out of the cab and yanking his pants up over his beer belly. It's against the regulations, he said in a gruff voice. At first I thought he was giving me a ticket, but it turned out to be a receipt. It turns out you have to pay to sleep on the ground—ten ducking follars, if you can believe it. He said, You know your license number? I made something up. It's a special POW plate, I told him. My dad parked it back by the creek. He looked where I pointed, then got back in his truck. Tell him to move it, he said, starting up the engine.

It was okay. That day, Saturday, was about the best day of my life, and I wish it had lasted forever because the next day, Sunday, was the worst—so far.

&
& &
&&&

In the middle of the night I had an asthma attack. I don't know what the temperature went down to, but when I crawled outside to go to the bathroom, the air on my butt was cold, and even the stars were shivering. All I had for covers was a pajama-party sleeping bag and an old lap robe that smelled like a dog had died in it.

My dad was pretty freaked out and wanted to drive me to the nearest emergency room. Asthma sounds a lot worse than it is, which is bad enough, and I was having a pretty severe attack. But it wasn't like I was going to die or anything. I had my Tedrol with me—it's just that it takes a while to work. For about half an hour he knelt there with his hands clasped in front of him like a worried kangaroo, while I leaned back on my outstretched arms, trying between gasps to explain that any minute I'd be all right.

Eventually, of course, the pill worked and I went back to sleep, though I kept waking up because of the damp and the cold. I think I may have frozen my patoogies off, because next morning I couldn't find them in their usual place. (That, by the way, is a sample of my mother's sick humor. When I was little she would say, Oh, it's so cold we're going to freeze our patoogies off. And then when we got back to the house, she'd say, See, no patoogies. All gone. No wonder I turned out the way I did. I always half assumed a patoogie was a penis.)

Next morning we crawled out of the tent to discover that some animal had knocked our trash can over and spread our garbage around for all the world to see. Also my towel, which I had hung out to dry, was sopping wet. The johns were about ten miles up the road. I have to be honest: I was a little pissed at my dad. The weather wasn't his fault, but he could at least have brought real sleeping bags or gotten us a room at a lodge or something. I mean, aside from the fact that *I* was probably catching my death of cold, camping late in August can't be all that healthy for a man in *his* condition. Just because he's a vet and wounded, you can't not be mad at your dad if he does something dumb. Because of what happened afterwards, I feel guilty now, but that was my attitude at the time. I'm trying to be honest.

The women's john smelled of disinfectant, which usually means they're trying to cover up something gross like herpes or AIDS. I could hardly see my face in the mirror because the only light was one of those fluorescent jobs that would come on for about a second and then flicker out. Needless to say, there was a dead bird in the sink. I was afraid to go to the bathroom with it lying there, all rigid and sleek, but finally I covered it with about ten paper towels. Luckily there was toilet paper. I guess I should have counted my blessings, but then I went to take a shower and no hot water came out.

I'm standing naked in the shower stall, I can feel myself getting athlete's foot, and the hot water won't turn on. Then I noticed this little sign that says FOR HOT WATER DEPOSIT 25¢. I hobbled out on my heels, found my jeans—I just knew the ranger was going to appear with his mops, though luckily he didn't. Amazingly enough, I had a quarter. I ran back to the stall, stuck it in the slot, got all ready for a nice hot shower. The thing even started to tick. But when I went to turn on the hot water, ice cubes came out. Ice cubes isn't a cold-enough description. I kept crowding against the wall, expecting it to warm up, but every time I put my elbow in to test it, I froze my patoogies off. I *had* to have a shower, take my word for it, so finally I just ran under, counted to ten, and ran out again. I almost had another asthma attack.

Then I scurried out into the anteroom, and naturally the towel my dad had lent me had dragged on the floor so that the end was all sandy and wet. I figured it was probably contaminated and all my children would be born with six toes.

While I was getting dressed, I heard my dad beating a tattoo on the wooden steps—*ra-ta-tat-a, ra-ta-tat-a, ra-ta-ta-a-tat!* That's when I realized that, Vietnam War or no Vietnam War, I was pissed at him! I let the screen door whap shut behind me and marched down the steps. He beat another flourish and looked up at me with laughing eyes.

Dumb monster. Another thing: my hair was wet and tangled because I had forgotten to bring a comb along. I set off for the campsite.

He caught up with me and tapped me on the shoulder. He was nodding and going through the motions of taking a shower. He looked about as smart as the Scarecrow in *The Wizard of Oz.*

I really didn't want to talk about it, but I explained how there wasn't any hot water.

He tapped me on the shoulder again, this time looking all concerned, and offered me a quarter.

"I put a quarter in. It started ticking. But no hot water came out."

He stopped me by putting one hand on my shoulder and gesturing with the other, like he was trying to explain something.

"I put the quarter in the right place. Where else would it go?"

He shook his head and made these really weird wiggling motions with his fingers. I had to watch while he drew a diagram in the dirt.

I shouted, "I don't understand what you're saying! You're supposed to turn the little gizmo back to START? You really think that had anything to do with it? Well, how am I supposed to know? They could at least have put a sign up."

He wanted me to go back and try again. To this end he did something I did not appreciate: he put his hand to his face and pinched his invisible nose, as if to say, P.U.

I stalked ahead, shouting, *"I took a blankety-blank cold shower, if you really want to know!"*

As soon as we got back to our campsite, I went inside the tent to comb the knots out of my hair. Then I tried to go back to sleep, which isn't that easy after you've just taken a freezing shower and your hair's still wet and you've just hollered at your father for something that you know isn't really his fault. I lay on my back, staring at a giant daddy longlegs that had somehow gotten into the tent and was celebrating by bouncing up and down on its skinny legs.

My dad probably thought I was soft and spoiled. That

made me even madder: I'm not soft and spoiled!

Meanwhile, he was out there banging pots and pans, playing the martyr, and pretty soon I heard a little scratching sound at the nylon window just above my head. I looked up: there was old E.T. Eyes, watching me sadly, holding something steaming in a cup. Come and get it, he said, tapping a spoon against the plastic cup.

Cute, I thought. Real cute.

I changed my socks, put my shoes on, tied the laces in a double knot. The front of the tent caught on the cuff of my pants, and I almost yanked the whole tent down kicking myself free. Once again my dad showed the delicacy and tact of Frankenstein, by covering his eyes with his hand.

I gave him what my mom calls my blue look.

I don't know what my blue look looks like exactly, since when a person's mad they don't usually run to look at themselves in the mirror. I'm aware of narrowing my eyes, which my mom says makes them flash blue like one of those lights on top of a police car.

Sometimes when people see it, they shrivel up and die, but not my dad. He just went on sitting there, holding his cup in both hands like he was Vietnamese or something.

While I stood there, he held up a plate that had eggs all over it like so many eyes. I looked at them; they looked at me. There was no way I was going to eat those pus sacks.

He patted the table to get my attention. This time he wanted to pour me a cup of coffee. Now I don't want you to think I'm a finicky eater. I like garlic, for example, unlike half the kids in my class. Also Greek olives. But I've never understood how anyone could eat a hen's period, which is what an egg is, after all, and coffee always reminds me of—I better not say what.

"No, thanks," I said. Or possibly I said, "Yuk, where's the orange juice?"

He started looking, too, under the cups and plates. Then I remembered we hadn't gotten any. Great. It was about forty degrees out, I was walking around in just a sweatshirt, and we didn't have any orange juice. (I happen to believe in vitamin C.)

I said I'd have milk and had just started towards the car to get it when he whacked the table a couple of times with the flat of his hand—really hard, so that everything bounced. He had the milk there.

He poked around until he found a semiclean cup, then started scooping the dead bugs or whatever out of it. Meanwhile, I was dying of thirst, so I grabbed the carton and held it over my mouth. I'm not crazy about milk, but I drink it for the protein and vitamin D.

I can't tell you how adorable my dad looked all of a sudden, all worried and confused, and I realized I wasn't mad at him anymore. Just the opposite: I wanted to make up.

Some of the milk was trickling down my chin and throat, so, without even meaning to, almost, I started blowing bubbles.

My dad just sat there, quietly drinking his coffee. Now he was the one being a grump.

I don't know what came over me. I started prancing around and put my arms around him and kissed him on the forehead.

He didn't put his arms around me or kiss me back. He just waited until I was through. Then he poured himself another cup of coffee like I wasn't even there.

Someone's little boy got up on the wrong side of the bed. That's what my mom used to say to my former stepdad,

Barry Comstock, when he was in a bad mood about something.

The sun came out. It was starting to get warmer. I wiped my mouth on the sleeve of my sweatshirt and scrunched the bacon up inside a piece of plain bread (because the toast was all burnt) and put the whole thing in my mouth, which made my cheeks puff out. Then I wiped the side of my mouth with my thumb and my thumb on my pants and started dancing and chewing.

He waited until I had swallowed.

The next thing I knew, he was on his feet. He grabbed me from behind and tripped me to the ground. In one second he was kneeling over me, shaking his fist in my face. I didn't know what to think: I hardly knew this man. What if he wasn't my father? What if he tried to spank me?

But he didn't. He just rolled over and sat up and looked extremely unhappy. Then he shook my shoulder and, while I watched, wrote B-R-A-T on the ground. I noticed he was taking deep breaths, his chest moving in and out.

He was staring away from me.

I'm not sure exactly why, but in that moment I loved him better than I ever had before, and I wanted more than anything in the world for him to love me back. When he glanced at me again, I couldn't help smiling at him. I felt like I was in love with him almost. He slowly shook his head, not in an angry way, and let out a sigh. Then he got to his feet and helped me to mine. Together we washed the dishes and packed up.

I won't tell you all the stuff we did that day, like visit his grave, where someone had planted a bunch of American flags in front of his tombstone. Secretly I kept hoping that he would take me back to the little town in Michigan he was from. To the farmhouse, still standing, where he and my mom met.

In all these years my grandmother has never sold it because it's been in the family so long. I think her mom, or her mom's mom, came out here in a covered wagon, back in the days of *Little House in the Big Woods*. It's been in the family ever since.

Grandma has this idea it would make a nice summer place. I used to try to get my mom to take me there, but for her it's just a barbarian wilderness, miles away from the nearest single-parent support group. Plus, of course, it has a lot of unhappy memories.

My Uncle Jimmy and his bowling buddies go up there once in a while, though according to my mom all they ever do is smoke cigars and play gin rummy. And tell dirty jokes, knowing my Uncle Jimmy.

Anyway, it was late in the afternoon. I was sitting there, not saying much, partly because, like I said, I hoped he was taking me to our old house, and I wanted to be able to act surprised when we went up the legendary hill and stopped at the gate my mom used to always tell me about.

Also, to be honest, I was thinking about my true love.

You didn't know I had a true love, did you? Well, you're right, he's not true. As far as that goes, I'm not really in love with him anymore, either.

Let's just say that I was thinking about someone I am trying not to think about. Someone I'm trying to fall out of love with, which is not as easy as it sounds. In a lot of ways you're better off being a priest. I'd probably become a nun myself if it weren't too late already.

This one headshrinker I went to said that every time I looked at B.'s photograph I should think of dog doo. Or put my finger down my throat.

I'm not kidding.

Whereas I was thinking of how he could make me laugh all the time, even when I was in a bad mood. Even then the thought of him made me smile—I couldn't help it. So, to make a long story short, I started thinking about him in all the ways I had decided not to, remembering both the good and the bad, wondering what he was thinking about everything and if there wasn't some way we could get back together. . . .

I picked up the map, idly. Usually I let myself be driven places without bothering to figure out where we are. But according to the map and the way the signs were pointing, we were headed southeast. Southeast? I looked at my dad and said, "I certainly hope you're not planning to drive all night in order to get me back to suburban Washington in time for when my parents get back from couple counseling, because if you are, I can tell you right now there's no way I'm ever going back to that *cul*-de-sac." I said, "Dad, I want to go where you're going. I want to live with you. We need each other, Dad."

I told him that while I loved my mom, I had reached the age when I needed a father—my real honest-to-God father.

"You could teach me more than any dumb school," I said. And in fact, I was hoping he would teach me everything he knew and let me be sort of his sidekick, which is a bigger concession than you might realize, since I haven't told you my feminist beliefs yet.

But to everything I said, he just shook his head, not really listening. God, it's amazing how fast men start acting like your father, telling you what's for your own good! As if *they* know. I happen to be in a much better position than anyone else to know whether suburban Washington and Mr. S. Leicester (Les) Smith are good for me or not!

We were driving through this little town in southern Michigan. The light turned red. My dad stopped, and I opened the door and got out.

I can't tell you exactly what I had in mind, because I wasn't sure myself, but half the time with so-called adults you have to do something dramatic or they don't pay attention. I stuffed my hands in my pockets like I was really pissed and started up the sidewalk. When the light changed, my dad drove alongside me, slowly, making that obnoxious gesture with the index finger that means, Get over here, young lady. I gave him my blue look and kept on walking.

Behind him there was an old lady in a Ford LTD who

could barely see over the dashboard, let alone go around, and she was too timid to honk. My dad saw her, too, in his rearview mirror. He jerked the gearshift and, the next thing I knew, he was growling up the street.

At first I expected him to just turn around and come back, but minutes passed and there was no sign of him. Maybe he just wanted to teach me a lesson? I walked around for a while, sort of glancing nonchalantly over my shoulder every few seconds. The stores were starting to close. In one of the windows I saw a pleasingly plump teenage girl with stringy hair, wearing old jeans and a red sweatshirt. Me, in other words. I looked like a runaway.

I walked over to the curb and looked at all the cars that passed, but they were all late models, nothing from the 50s or 60s. For a second, as I was standing there, I had this strange sensation that my mom could see me, though of course that was silly. She was hundreds of miles away.

But then, because *no one* could see me, or if they did, could care less, I went inside a Laundromat and called Barry Comstock, my former stepfather.

Actually, I might as well tell you I had a pocketful of quarters saved up for just such an occasion, i.e., for when I just happened to be walking by a public phone and didn't have time to think about whether it was a smart thing to do or not. And now my wish was coming true, and my heart was going *ping, ping, ping,* along with the coins, as I dropped them one by one into the coin slot. And before I even had a chance to work out what I was going to say, the phone was ringing on the other end, much louder than I wanted it to. I remember thinking, This is it, now or never.

Then he said, Hello! in this really cheerful voice. And like a big dummy, I said, Hi, it's me, Elizabeth—like I really thought he'd be happy to hear from me, duh. And then, Father Jude, there followed the longest, awkwardest pause I've ever heard in my life, and finally he swallowed and said, What number are you calling? his voice so strained I almost didn't recognize it. And like the complete ninny I am to this day, I said, 1–603–555–9883, in other words, *my old number.* And he said, I think the person you want doesn't live here anymore.

So after about ten seconds I got the message and hung up.

Sometimes I'm so dumb it makes me want to eat stones. I don't know why I thought he could be of more use to me than my real father who, when you stop and think about it, had to overcome incredible obstacles and travel God knows how far just to be with me, but there you have it. Deep down I must be a truly ignorant person.

Not to mention deceitful.

The sun had gone down, but it was still light out. The sky was baby blue. In the weeds between the buildings the crickets were chirping. If you've ever gotten out of a car in a strange town, then you know there's nothing lonelier than being by yourself, when just a few minutes before you were riding along comfortably with somebody else—although, strangely enough, it's *only* at times like that that I feel maybe I believe in God after all. Don't ask me why. I guess because being alone makes you feel small, so you want to believe in something *big*, someone you can rely on.

I was also wondering if this was my punishment for messing up everybody else's life, and if so, when it was okay to start praying for forgiveness?

At the end of the business section I turned down a side street that sloped downhill, past a drab brick wall with an iron fire escape, to the river. The river was as bright as the sky, while everything else was getting darker by the second. Across the river was a big factory or mill with about a hundred squares of yellow light. I sat down on the concrete whatever-you-call-it and leaned over the iron railing and spit.

It was easier not to think about Barry now. I could even be grateful to him for being clear about where we stood.

I tried to imagine what it would be like if I really did go home, if I just got on the next bus and called when I got into Washington. *But it went against everything I believe in.*

You must have realized by now, Father Jude, I've got problems I haven't even begun to tell you about yet, and if you want out now, it's okay with me and no hard feelings. I wouldn't blame you. I mean, I *want* to keep writing this and telling you everything, but the closer I get to the truth—to the gross parts—the harder it is.

By the way, before I left home, I looked in the yellow pages under Religions/Roman Catholic, because even then I was thinking of talking to a priest. But unfortunately all I got was a recording that said they were closed for the day and to leave a message or call back Tuesday. It said to say the Rosary.

So meeting you seemed providential.

I was sitting by the river, thinking my thoughts, and the more I thought about it, the more I realized I couldn't go back. Not then, not now. And that sooner or later I would have to tell my dad why, and he might not think as highly of me, but at least he'd have to let me stay.

So I prayed he'd come back. Which he did, though God made me wait a long time, almost an hour it felt like.

I looked up, and there he was, sitting on the other side of the river, staring at me. We were about twenty feet apart, I guess, and the evening sky was perfectly mirrored in the brimming water. It was like he just emerged from the shadows. Slowly he raised his hand over his shoulder and wiggled his fingers. I kicked the wall once with the backs of my sneakers.

"Hey," I called out. "Are you hungry, by any chance? Because I'm starving."

I could just barely make him out: He was nodding.

"There's a place over there where we can get pizza. You like pizza?"

He kept on nodding.

I was on the verge of telling him across that space that I was sorry for acting like a nine-year-old. But instead I started tilting my head this way and that and smiling my wouldn't-you-like-to-know-what-I'm-thinking smile—which was exactly how I *didn't* want to act! I thought, Here I go again.

So I got up and started walking along the river, which was getting to be the color of night, and as I walked I hit the tops of all the metal posts with my open hand—hard, so it hurt—and my dark shadow over on the other side of the river started walking along, too, hitting his hand, as I *knew he would.*

Then I started running, as fast as I could, up the hill to the bridge and across, and threw my arms around his neck, dancing in place on my tiptoes, and blubbering, "I'm sorry, I'm sorry, I'm sorry, I'm sorry," and other stuff hard for anyone else to decipher because I prefer to mumble my apologies and declarations of love.

I told him I was bad news—he leaned away and shook his head. You're not bad news, he said. You're your father's pride and joy. (Aren't I a good translator?)

"I'll go back if you really want me to," I said, "but . . ."

To which he made no reply. Maybe he already had some inkling of what was going to happen.

It was later the same night. I held a slice of pizza towards the windshield. "Loog, Dag," I said with my mouth full of cheese. "A fair!"

My dad swung into the crowded parking lot, which by day must have been someone's meadow, and turned the engine off.

I said, "You want to?"

His eyes said, If you do, so I rummaged in the back to find a jacket to put on over my sweatshirt. Then, bouncing out of the car, I hooked my arm through his, and we went in at the lighted gate.

I forgot to say that in Grand Rapids we went to a novelty shop and bought him a James Dean mask, which was what he was wearing. People looked at us a little funny, but since it was a fair it didn't matter that much. They probably thought we were advertising something.

Under the carnival lights the grass looked like it does in the daytime, almost. You could see individual faces in the crowd, teenagers huddled into gangs, trying to look cool—looking cold instead, the boys shivering in their fancy silk shirts. I felt sorry for them. I was glad I had my dad with me.

44

I couldn't seem to stop jumping up and down. "Oh, the Whoosh!" I cried. "You want to go on the Whoosh?"

My dad turned his James Dean face up at the Whoosh. He didn't exactly nod his head up and down. Me, I couldn't seem to stand still. I don't know what had come over me. I felt like an orphan on her yearly spree.

I told him how my Cousin Janet and I had gone on the Whoosh at Coney Island a couple of summers ago. "It's a wicked ride. You'll see. I laughed so hard I almost wet my pants."

We had wandered over to the machine in question and were standing just outside its swooping lights.

"My cousin and I went on it six times. It's neat. See, it goes round and round, higher and higher—then it goes *whoosh!*"

Just then the machine went *whoosh*, letting out a huge mechanical, if you'll forgive me for saying so, fart. The little cars, which were attached to the ends of long white spokes, dropped fifteen feet or so, shaking screams of laughter into the night.

"Don't you want to try? It's a lot of fun."

He was looking at me kind of doubtfully. We strolled past the beanbag toss, where a kid with a yellow mohawk was trying to win a Kewpie doll for his spike-haired date. The huckster beckoned for us to try next, but we shook our heads and kept on walking. We went as far as the wagon belonging to the Headless Woman Who Is Still Alive, then turned back.

Somehow we ended up back at the Whoosh.

A new group had just piled into the swinging chairs. Slowly at first, the machine wound them up, like it had the first batch. Then—*whoosh*—it dropped them just above our heads. Laughter spilled over us. Somewhere scratchy circus music was playing.

> Lump, da dee da,
> Lump, da dee da.

The night was all spangly bright. My dad must have felt the magic, because he took out his wallet.

"Way to go!" I said, snatching some dollars and running off to buy the tickets. While I was standing in line, I waved to him, but he had wandered into the shadow of the Whoosh and didn't see me.

I ran back with the tickets in my teeth, happy as a retard, and in another half a minute it was our turn to go crowding up the gangplank. My dad steadied the little car while I climbed in, then he got in after me. Pretty soon a man with a soldier's raw face, looking kind of crazed around the eyes, came along and locked the bar kind of roughly across our laps.

At first nothing happened. The car swayed like a porch swing. I felt like I was Julie Harris in my all-time favorite movie, *East of Eden.* Then we started to move. I squeezed my dad's hand. He had his head pressed against the back of the seat, watching the night rise up around us. Up there you could see it really *was* night out. The lights below were only glitter.

Gradually we picked up speed, which meant I was thrown rather heavily against my dad; we were both being squeezed against his side of the car. It occurred to me that if one of the bolts that was holding us in came loose, we would fly about a mile in the air before crashing to the hard ground. But luckily none of the bolts came loose.

The machine was going faster now, higher and higher. I

screamed at the top of my lungs, "Isn't this fun? Wonder when it *whooshes*?"

Then. Out of the night we plummeted back into the bubble of lights below with only the bar across our laps to hold us in, and then the ground fell away again and we were being jerked back up into the dark and there were tears in my eyes, swept by the wind across my face. I shouted, "Isn't this fun? Isn't this the most fun you've ever had?"

But my dad was holding the bar with both hands, his knuckles hard and white. His eyes, wide open, glittered with panic. And either he or the wind was making a low moaning sound.

Oh my God, I thought, he's going to have a heart attack, all because of me. Here against all probabilities he had survived the war only to be killed by his own daughter.

I prayed God would make us stop, or if one of us had to go, to let it be me this time. My own stomach was beginning to feel unhappy.

When we swooped past the cabin, I shouted, "Could we please stop, please. There's a sick person on board."

But either they didn't hear me or the wheel just wasn't ready to stop yet. The sky and lights kept whooshing by.

After about a hundred years, heaven and earth finally slowed down, we dropped matter-of-factly back into the busy carnival, and stopped.

I threw off the bar, helped my dad stagger down the gangplank onto terra firma, where he started groping for grass like a blind man. Next thing I knew, he was sitting on the ground, his head still going round in orbit.

I knelt beside him. "I'm sorry, Dad," I kept saying. "Are you going to be all right and everything? I remember it as being more fun than that, honest."

He was hitting at the bottom of his mask like he couldn't breathe, and when I yanked it up over his face, he toppled over backwards in a faint.

You would have thought that people would have reacted. That at least somebody would have screamed or said, "Oh my God in heaven, they must have fallen from the Ferris wheel! Somebody, quick, get an ambulance!"

But like a bunch of sheep all they did was just step over us like we weren't writhing on the grass.

"It's all right," I told him. "People never want to get involved."

I helped him to his feet. "He's a Vietnam vet," I called over my shoulder to people who were giving me weird looks. "He got wounded in the war. Let us through, please."

My dad was very unsteady on his feet, so I put his arm around me and steered him towards the wagon of the Headless Woman Who Is Still Alive. Just behind her wagon was an ordinary meadow. A few steps, and we were out of the fairgrounds. My dad put his hands on his thighs and started heaving up his supper. This was a pretty gross sight, so I'll spare you the details, but just imagine.

To tell you the truth, I didn't feel so hot myself. I distinctly remember thinking that I *did not* want to see the Headless Woman Who Is Still Alive. My dad kept motioning for me to go away, but I was afraid to let go of him. I sacrificed my jacket to clean some of the puke off.

"Come on," I said. "Let's get out of here."

By staying on the dark side of the wagons, we were able to circle the fairgrounds without running into anybody, except for this boy and girl who were too busy doing I-won't-say-what to care one way or the other. My dad "said" he was okay enough to drive, though he had trouble starting the car. There was a loud crash beyond the trees—thunder, I realized. There was another rumble coming. People started running, screaming with laughter, trying to make it back to their cars before the rain came down.

We drove and drove, while all around us lightning crackled and thunder boomed. Usually I like storms, but that night in the backwoods of central Michigan I scooted over next to my dad and didn't mind it one bit when he put his arm around me and held me close, even though we both smelled of vomit. The rain was coming down in curtains. The wipers would take a swipe at it, and in a second the windshield would be flooded again. I tried to sing a song to cheer us up, but then we went whooshing through this puddle and the car made a funny noise. The headlights dimmed and went out.

I sat up as we coasted onto the soggy shoulder and stopped. I looked at my dad, he looked at me. He turned the key, but nothing happened. He tried again. Nothing. He waited a minute, then held the key for about ten seconds, but it was no use. I don't know that much about cars, but I think his wires must have gotten wet. Way off there were muffled booms of thunder. Then suddenly right over our heads lightning exploded. My dad went rigid. For about five seconds the world looked like a black-and-white TV program. Then everything grew dark again. He didn't move, except I felt his hand extend to mine.

We sat there holding hands like a couple of kids at a drive-in movie.

"Maybe a car will come by," I said, looking out all the windows. "Does it sound to you like it's letting up? Dad, look! Is that a cottage? I could ask to use their phone. I could call a tow truck."

Standing back away from the road, something gleamed in the trees. It might have been a cottage. My dad wasn't doing a very good job of communicating with me. I don't know what had come over him. Every time lightning struck, he twisted his shoulders and jerked his head.

I watched him for a while, then I said, "I'll be right back." Putting both hands on the handle, I shoved out into the rain. I headed straight back under the dripping trees. There was no car in the gravel driveway, no smoke rising from the chimney, no lights on inside. The only sign of life was a bedraggled-looking cat who came hurrying out from under the porch, meowing.

"Hello!" I shouted, banging on the front door. "Anybody home?"

The front door was locked. I cupped my hands to the window, then, hearing a noise, wheeled around to see something awful limping towards me.

But it was only him.

"You scared me!" I cried, letting out a shriek of laughter.

A car came slickering out of the night. I raced back to the road just in time to watch its pink taillights evaporate around the bend. Standing in the middle of the road, I tilted my head back and opened my mouth to the rain. There comes a time when you're already soaked, anyway, so you might as well try to enjoy it.

I frog-hopped back to the cottage—where I found my dad, looking more shell-shocked than ever, holding open the front door.

"How'd you get in?"

He pointed around to the back.

"Anyone home?"

He shook his head.

I took off my shoes and socks in the front hall and wiped my feet on the braided rug in the living room. Then, stealing from room to room, knocking first, looking under the beds, checking the closets to make sure, I ascertained that the place was ours. My dad followed on noiseless feet, holding on to my shirt.

"See? No one's home. There's nothing to worry about. It looks like no one's been here for ages."

The cottage was furnished with secondhand furniture, like whoever owned it only used it in the summer. In one corner of the refrigerator we found a shrunken apple and half a can of moldy corn. A few old clothes hung in the bedroom closet—a gray sweater full of holes, a granny dress like my mom used to wear. Plus there was a cardboard box full of old shoes. The toilet bowl filled with rust-colored water when I flushed it. The bed had just a thin maroon spread over it, no sheets.

Over my shoulder I said, "This can be our house." But when I turned around, he wasn't there.

I found him in the kitchen, squatting in a corner, shivering. The cat was between his knees, licking his wet socks. "Are you okay?" I asked. "We'd better put on some dry clothes or you'll catch your death of cold. I'll try to find something for us to eat."

I stooped down to help him and ended up on the floor, sort of holding him against my bosom. To tell you the truth, I'd never thought of it as a bosom before. I rocked him for a while, humming and singing verses from "Blowin' in the Wind," which I figured was from his era. After a while he started breathing normally.

I got up and went into the bathroom. Hot water poured from the tap, but I didn't really think about it. I went and got my dad and helped him peel off his wet clothes. Then I gave him a hand as he stepped into the tub. He kept looking around like he wasn't sure where he was, like it had been a long time since he had taken a bath, like he had forgotten how to sit down in one. His body was incredibly emaciated, if it isn't a sin for a daughter to know that about her own father, and he had other scars I hadn't seen before, including a pink gash on his side.

"You sit there and relax," I said, kneeling on the floor. He kept staring at his knees, which rose like barren islands above the steaming water. I reached across him for the soap and began making lather. He turned his empty face to me, and I dabbed soapsuds on the raw skin. I washed his shoulders and back. When I was through, he patted my hand.

"There," I said, rocking back on my heels. "You can do the rest. I'll call you when supper's ready."

In the mirror above the sink I caught sight of a slightly more drawn, older-looking me. And behind me, the empty tub of water. My dad's explained more than once why because of what happened to him in Vietnam you can't see his reflection in any mirror, but I'm hopeless when it comes to science. I still don't get it.

I had to run back out to the car and get his overnight bag, which had dry clothes in it. I put it just inside the bathroom door. He had slouched down in the tub, so that only his head was visible, a sight impossible to describe.

I hurried next door, to the bedroom, and put on the dress and the sweater that were hanging in the closet, looping a string of wooden beads around my neck. I had my own dry clothes in the car, but if there's a chance to play dress-up, I can never resist, and besides the granny dress was a relief for my middle. It took a while to find shoes that fit. The first pair I tried on were too big, the next too small, and so forth. But finally at the bottom of the pile I found some gloppy men's boots that were just right, ha ha.

Then I remembered the cat, which wasn't that hard since he kept darting at my ankles. I scooped him up and carried him, purring so hard I could feel it against my chest, back into the kitchen.

53

All I could find in the cupboards was a can of Campbell's pea soup and half a bag of popcorn, but this was a stroke of luck because soup and popcorn are two of the things I know how to cook. It took some more rummaging through drawers to come up with a can opener and some pans, but pretty soon I had the soup bubbling and the popcorn popping. You could smell the popcorn all through the house. The cat, by the way, had gulped down his share of the pea soup and was already looking up for more.

Even before I shouted "Come and get it," I could hear my dad moving around.

&
& &
&   &
&   &
&&&&

Pea soup and popcorn aren't that bad a combination when you're starving, and we had all the fresh water we could drink. For dessert, I served sugarless gum, since I always carry a pack of sugarless gum in my purse, only of course—duh—my dad can't chew gum. We were both warm and dry by now. The cat was pushing the soup pan around the kitchen.

My dad insisted on sleeping in the sleeping bag on the

floor, which meant the cat and I got the bed. I felt a little guilty about this arrangement, but he claimed he had gotten used to sleeping on the floor in Vietnam.

We turned the light out, and I chattered and shivered under my solitary blanket until, by degrees, I felt myself getting warmer and starting to drift off to sleep. One of Barry's favorite sayings occurred to me, If two lie together they are warm; how can one be warm alone? He's full of sayings like that.

Just before I conked out, I had the same sensation that my mom could see me, that she was somehow in the room, watching me. But when I lifted my head to look, there was just us: me and the cat, who also lifted his head.

And also my dad, of course, lying motionless on the floor.

I guessed everything would be all right and lay back down.

The next thing I was aware of, a woman was saying, Fred, come back. We should wait for the police.

I could hear the back door being opened slowly. A light was moving through the house.

I sat up in bed. "Dad!" I whispered. "Somebody's here."

He didn't move. Then I saw the sleeping bag was empty.

"Dad?" I said in my normal voice. Then louder, almost shouting, I'm in here. Our car got stuck, and we were stranded. We're not hippies. Hi. My dad's around here someplace. Don't be scared if he looks bad. He was wounded in the war. He's very gentle—he wouldn't hurt a fly. We ate your soup and popcorn. We were going to pay you back.

There were people standing in the doorway. They were shining a light in my eyes.

```
        &
       &&&
      &&&&&
    &&&&&&&
    &        &
    & HELP!  &
    &&&  &&&
```

&

Dad? Somebody?

Help! What am I supposed to do now?

I had a nightmare when I was still in the hospital. If there'd been someone there I knew or trusted, I would have gone and gotten in bed with them. As it was, I got out of bed and went and stood in the john down the hall until I was sure the coast was clear. Then I tiptoed past the sleeping nurse, leaned softly on the exit door that led to the stairs, and two seconds later I was running like aitch-ee-double-hockey-sticks across the empty parking lot.

I dreamt I was seeing a Vietnam War movie. Up on the

screen there was this road quivering in the moonlight with corpses strewn all over the place, including a dog or a pig with its legs sticking straight up in the air. Also, I don't want to make you sad or anything, but there was this smooshed-up baby buggy with a baby inside. Her foot was sticking out.

At first nothing happened, everything was still. Then one of the supposedly dead soldiers blinked his glassy eyes and sat up. He staggered to his feet like a zombie, got the baby, and headed straight into the jungle.

I knew something awful was going to happen, the way it always does in Vietnam movies: Just when you least expect it, tiny choppers appear on the horizon or a machine gun opens fire—*ra-ta-ta-a-tat*. But for what seemed like the longest time, the soldier with the baby on his shoulder just kept hacking vines and branches with his army knife. All you could hear was someone having trouble breathing and the swishing sound that a person makes when they move through vegetation.

Finally, just as dawn was breaking, he reached a clearing, and on the other side of a rice paddy that reflected the morning clouds, there was this perfectly intact peasant village with no burnt-out hootches or dead people with their guts splattered all over the place.

So naturally I braced my knees against the empty seats in front of me and closed my eyes. But all I could hear was the soldier just calmly splish-splashing through the rice paddy, and when I opened them again he was standing up to his boots in water, trying to give the baby a bath. She had begun to give off a peculiar odor—which I could smell, sitting in the empty theater—and it was like he thought it was just vomit or something you could wash off.

She was dead, of course. She had been dead all along—either that, or she died of her wounds during the night.

But he carefully undid her charred little *ao dai* and dipped his bandanna into the water, and when he was done sponging her off as best he could, he held her naked body up to the sun to dry. Then he carried her into one of the huts and tried to make her lie flat on a straw mat. Flies kept coming out of the corners of her eyes.

The soldier plopped down next to her like a heavy sack and broke out some C rations, some ham and beans, which he started eating greedily in fingerfuls, only every once in a while he would fish out a nice plump bean or a little chunk of meat and try to push it into her snapping-turtle mouth. Finally, when the can was empty, he covered her with his army shirt and lay down on his back.

And still nothing scary happened.

For the longest time they just lay there, side by side. Then slowly they started shriveling up like stuff you leave in the refrigerator too long. At first when I was waking up, I was relieved that there hadn't been the usual sex and violence, but still I felt like something was wrong. Then suddenly my heart went *boom, boom, boom,* and before I had time to really think about what I was doing, I was outdoors in the fresh air, running or walking as fast as my bronchial tubes would let me.

& &

In a way I'm sorry I took off when I did, because I was about to write down what was really up.

I had gotten as far as that fateful night when the Twemlows came home and found me asleep in their bed like Goldilocks. *This is the truth:* They stood, huddled together in the bushes, while I was being escorted to the police car, and I had to shout over the voices on the radio that we were sorry for trespassing and would gladly repay them for anything we had used. I even offered to mow their lawn for the next hundred years—ha ha—but they didn't laugh or smile. They stood there with the blue light flashing in their frightened eyes like I was a mass murderer or something.

On the way to the police station I leaned my arms on the back of the front seat and tried telling the arresting officers that my dad suffered from post-traumatic stress disorder and that I had to go look for him in the woods, quick—*since he might be in danger or something!*

But you could tell they didn't believe a word I said. This one officer who combed his hair up in front like Ronald Reagan said they hadn't seen any signs of a second individual and that there would have been tire tracks on the shoulder (which was his polite way of saying that I'm a liar).

He held a printed card up to the dome light and read me my rights.

I have the right to remain silent? I thought, sitting back in the seat. Needless to say, I stopped talking then and there, and haven't said a word since.

At first I felt kind of mean because they were only doing their job and being extremely patient, and one of them had blond peach fuzz on his arms, although naturally he was wearing a wedding ring. But I know from experience that once you admit to people that you can talk, they start trying to persuade you to go against your beliefs. Whereas, if you don't talk, they're powerless against you.

Also I didn't want to start blabbing until I had my story straight.

At the police station, which was in the basement of the courthouse, they kept me waiting in the lobby for at least an hour while they filled out a report on me and got the chief or whatever-you-call-it out of bed. Then I had to go into his office like I'd been a bad girl, and for about half an hour or so he tried to persuade me to say who I was and where I came from. It was all I could do to keep from laughing because he looked exactly like the French policeman in *Casablanca*. I'm not kidding. We know you can talk, he said, blowing his nose in his handkerchief. You're only making it harder on everybody, including yourself.

Which may be true since everybody says the same thing, but I don't give a poopnod. They should let me go, since I said I was sorry and didn't hurt anyone.

But just because I refused to tell them who I was, etc., they took me back outside to where the same officers were waiting, and this time they drove me to the county hospital, which is sad because I would have preferred to go home with Peach Fuzz. By now it was getting to be morning out, but I had to see the county headshrinker, who wasn't amused by any of my quote unquote shenanigans, especially since I wouldn't tell him whether our insurance pays for psychiatric care on an emergency basis.

Needless to say, I just sat there, letting my tongue sort of dart out at the side of my mouth and making monkey noises.

Then this red-haired nurse took me up to the loony bin, and I had to fill out a questionnaire. Where it said name, I put down *Iphigenia,* and for religion, I lied and said *Catholic.* And where it asked if I wanted to be visited by a clergyman, I wrote *Yes, please!*

Finally they let me sleep, and I slept for about a hundred years until this other nurse who looked like someone had stepped on the middle of her face came in and plopped a tray on my lap. It was supposed to be my lunch: a piece of dead cow. I poked it with my knife, wishing I was a vegetarian, only I hate vegetables. Then the door opened again, and this time a priest stuck his head in and said, Knock, knock.

Hi, I'm Father Jude, he said, coming in and shutting the door behind him. I hope I'm not disturbing you.

He looked right at me and smiled and said, I'm supposed to ask you what's up, but I figure if you have anything to tell me, you will when you're good and ready, right?

I didn't say anything, so he sat down in the visitor's chair and sighed and started telling me about *his* father, who was downstairs on the old people's ward. Apparently he's an alcoholic. To tell the truth, I never thought of priests as having parents before, though of course they'd have to, duh.

(Top secret, *do not read:* I like Father Jude. Not *boing!*—

but someone you would definitely like to hug and vice versa. I *don't* mean that the way it sounds, but I can't help wondering why all the cool men in the world are either married or else they're priests—ha ha.)

Anyway, he went on talking, mostly about his father, who he kept calling Pop. And then finally he got around to me and said that if I had proof my father existed, like a letter or something, the Twemlows wouldn't press charges because Mr. Twemlow was also a vet—he was in the Pacific during World War II.

But that if I was involved in drugs or anything like that, they wanted me prosecuted to the full extent of the law. Then he goes, You and I know that's not what this is all about.

Later in the evening he came back and gave me this notebook, which he bought in the gift shop downstairs. If I didn't feel like talking, he said, I could write to him. And it would just be between us. That's a promise, he said, patting my feet where they stuck up under the covers.

So as soon as he left, I started writing, I wrote and wrote, and I'm still writing. It's like I'm afraid to stop.

&
& &

I couldn't get the nightmare out of my mind. Were they both really dead the whole time?

Every time I heard a car coming, I quickly went and stood behind a tree or a telephone pole or squatted down beside a garbage can.

If someone is dead, they're dead, like my Grandpa Topham whose head felt like a month-old pumpkin when I thought we were supposed to kiss him in the funeral parlor.

After a while it started to get light out, and I decided that by seven at the latest people would put two and two together, the nurse would go into my room and find the bed unmade, the doctor would call the police, and before I could even make it to the county line, they would be after me with their sirens blaring, to take me back to the hospital for the tests that the county headshrinker kept alluding to. What kind of tests, if I may ask? Can they really poke around in a person's innards without their permission?

So the next time I saw headlights coming, without even thinking, I dashed out in the middle of the street and started waving my arms up and down. Luckily it was just an old pickup truck. The driver had to swerve to avoid hitting me, but before he had a chance to roll down his window and say, What the #%!@ are you trying to do, young lady—get yourself killed? I was on the front seat next to him, rolling my eyes and moaning and saying I had to get to the nearest big town *quick!* because I was five months pregnant, and if you're going to have an abortion you have to do it before the end of your sixth month, which meant I only had twelve days to go!

He said a prayer out loud. He said, Dear Jesus, please show me the way to this young person's heart, while there is still time remaining. He said I'd be taking the life of one of God's beautiful creatures who had as much right to live as any of the rest of us. He said he and his wife had been asking the Lord for years to have a baby, but so far in His wisdom He had denied them.

(Don't they know that asking the Lord isn't enough?— ha ha.) He looked all right, I guess, in a droopy sort of way. I wasn't afraid of him or anything. But I think he's one of those right-wing nuts who are against abortion and think teenage girls should get pregnant just so they can have their children for them.

Still, I pretended to be very moved by his arguments. I wiped away my crocodile tears and told him that he was right, I could never in a million years kill my unborn child, however inconvenient it might be at this point in my life, and that I would go to a home for unwed mothers and either raise the child myself or else, when the time came, give it up for adoption, which moved him so much that he stopped at a roadside café and bought me a mountain of pancakes for breakfast. I felt a little guilty, but gobbled them down anyway.

&
&&&

It's twenty-four hours later. I'm writing this from Manistee, the heart (or pit?) of Michigan's cherry country. The sign on the door says I can stay here until 11:00 A.M. I won't be having pancakes for breakfast today, since I keep getting fatter as it is—ha ha. But for lunch I can get a tuna fish and pickle sandwich at a truck stop farther down the road and still have a fair amount of money left over. In the early afternoon, when hopefully all the state troopers are taking their siestas, I can hitch a ride with a truck driver whose face I trust, and by this time tomorrow, if I'm lucky, I'll be at least five states away.

I figured yesterday that I'd be safer off the streets for one night, so I stayed in this hotel, only believe me it isn't worth all the money they charge you. The room smells like the inside of an old suitcase, and I won't tell you what I found in the wastebasket. When I checked in, I told the lady at the desk that my dad was out parking the car and would be up later, but she obviously didn't care one way or the other. I think they only care if you make a lot of noise or break things.

At first I was too wide awake to go back to sleep, so I explored the closet and opened all the drawers, but all I found were four curled-up sheets of stationery with the hotel's name on them, plus a Bible, which I'm thinking of keeping since I've been meaning to read it, anyway, and whoever left it is obviously long gone.

And then, because I still get scared when I'm all by myself, I sat down at the skimpy desk they give you and started writing to Father Jude again, asking him to *pulease* not say anything to my mom about my dad coming back to life—if she should happen to track him down, which I wouldn't put past her—because she wouldn't in a million years believe a word I said. I know, I said, because we've been over this a million times. She wouldn't believe my dad was really alive if he was standing there before her very eyes because, although she has many sterling qualities, she's a woman of little faith about things like that—the only thing she believes in besides politics and abortion is getting into an Ivy League college. I told him that nobody in our family was very religious, and that the only time we ever prayed was at Thanksgiving, when it was more like a toast.

If my dad was standing there in the flesh, Mom would just calmly reach for the phone and dial the Pentagon, or her hero, Dan Rather of the "CBS Evening News," and say, Excuse me, Dan, but could you tell me if any MIAs from Vietnam have turned up unexpectedly? What about any secret congressional trips to Hanoi?

I said, I can joke about this because it doesn't threaten me, but can't you just imagine my dad, who's not used to the way she is now, fading into the walls?

I wrote other stuff, too, like that my mom knew the army hospital outside Valley Forge was closed down in the 70s. That we both knew because I really did use to write to a vet there who was badly wounded and supposed to have known my dad, only he never wrote back, probably because he was too far gone, and so on and so forth.

Luckily I didn't have a stamp at the time, because when I woke up this morning and reread the letter, I ripped it up and flushed it down the toilet. And it's a good thing I checked, because the toilets here are so pitiful that it took three flushes to get all the pieces of paper down. When I think that he might somehow have lifted up the seat and found some of the pages still floating around in the bowl and scooped them out and started reading that crap again—put it this way, at least he could have used the commode to barf in if he wanted to.

I asked to see a priest in the first place so I could finally tell someone everything and have them say, You poor thing, I really sympathize and will do everything I can to help you because I think you're very brave to be doing what you're doing, etc., but it was embarrassing because he's not only a priest, but also a man. I mean, there are certain things you don't want to have to tell someone of the opposite sex, no matter how holy they are.

Dear Father Jude,

How are you? I'm fine. I wrote you another letter, but it went astray. I'm sorry I had to leave without saying good-bye.

Good-bye!

I have to warn you. My mom is probably going to track you down, don't ask me how. And if you tell her any of what I told you, I can tell you right now she's going to try to prejudice you against me. I might as well come right out and say it. She thinks I'm crazy—well, not crazy, but . . .

She thinks I'm crazy because when I was a little kid I used to make pictures for my dad and bury them in the sandbox. I personally think that that's a perfectly normal way for a small child to react to a death in the family, but Mom decided it was a symptom of being schizo. I think she felt guilty for leaving me with baby-sitters all the time while she was starting her illustrious career. (I didn't mind the baby-sitters. They let me eat Froot Loops.)

Then when I was in the seventh grade, I wrote a paper for English called Letter to My Old Man. "Hey, Dad," it began.

> Long time no see. How's it going up there—I assume you're up, not down, ha ha. There's something I have to ask you. If you knew Mom was pregnant, how could you go off to Vietnam and get killed? I suppose I shouldn't be asking you stuff like that, but if you want to know the truth, it's caused us both no end of trouble.

I don't remember the exact words, and I admit it was a pretty smart-alecky thing to do, but I needed an *A* badly, and Miss Staplemeyer loved confessions—all you had to do was write about getting your period, and she thought you were some kind of literary genius. The last thing I expected was that she would show it to my mom, who immediately braved the homicidal Boston traffic—we were living in New Hampshire at the time—so I could be seen by the celebrated Dr. Peter Smilax with his beard like Sigmund Freud's, who said I was suffering from an Electra complex on a dead man.

(I ask you.)

"True! Nervous, very, very dreadfully nervous I had been and am; but why *will* you say that I am mad? The disease had sharpened my senses, not destroyed, not dulled them. . . . I heard all things in the heaven and in the earth. I heard many things in hell." Etc.

(I certainly hope you know where that's from. It's from "The Tell-Tale Heart" by Edgar Allan Poe.)

Oops—sorry about that. That was the maid, checking to see if the room was still occupied. She kept looking past me like she thought I had a man in here. Or a bong.

I pretended to be a little kabadocuckoo. I talked with my tongue hanging partway out. I thaid my dad wenth out to geth the paper, but that ath thoon ath he goth back, we wuth leaving, anyway. She kept saying she had twenty-four rooms to clean and wasn't going to hang around all day—like it was my fault she has such a crummy job.

Something tells me I better go. Like what if she goes downstairs and tells them the girl in Room 304 is all alone. I shouldn't have opened the door. I should have shouted, Who the hell is it! in a really angry voice.

I keep hearing this little kid out there who runs up and down the hall making airplane noises. I assume he's hers, because she's always shouting, "I'll smack you," though luckily she never does.

If she really wants him to stop, she should get him interested in something else or turn what they're doing into a game. I don't think she's very bright.

I guess that's not a nice thing to say about another person, but she's wearing a miniskirt to clean rooms in, which is exactly the sort of thing my friend Stacey would do.

Plus, she's not that attractive. In fact, she's kind of ugly. She looks like one of those animals you've never actually seen, but you can guess what they look like from their names, like weasel or ferret. She can't be more than eighteen, if that, and isn't wearing a wedding ring.

Suddenly I'm very depressed. I was going to tell you what was up, but now unfortunately I'm not in the mood.

Listen, do me one last favor. If my mom does find you, please tell her everything's fine, not to worry, etc., etc., but for the time being I have to be alone.

Good-bye, Father. Wish me luck, or bless me if you think I deserve it.

H
ow
I foun
d him a
gain&&&
&&&&&&&
&&& &&&

&

Wahaneeka, Michigan
September 5

When they go to make the movie of my life, this part has to be in black and white. Because when I got off the bus in Wahaneeka yesterday, it was already dark out, but way up in the clear gray sky a full moon was shining, and it's amazing how much light they give off. I could read where I had written my real name and telephone number on the back of my hand. Is it always like that, and I've just never noticed before? Even the weeds cast shadows. Even the cigarette butts.

It was also hot for a change—in the 80s, it felt like. There were insects doing loop-de-loops around the gas station lights. I asked the kid in the glass booth where you pay, if he knew where the Topham house was, because the place is still supposed to be in my grandmother's name, but he shook his head and said over the intercom, Sure don't.

It's okay, I said, waving, and in fact I wasn't worried. I've never been there—at least that I can remember—but my mom always said that once you get to Wahaneeka, you can't miss it. It stands on top of the only hill for miles around.

So I looked around to see if I could tell which way was up, only everything in the state of Michigan seems pretty level to me.

I haven't said that much in the last few days, and when I spoke to the guy in the booth, the sound of my own voice startled and disgusted me. It sounded like a little kid's voice. I was afraid he would think I was one of those teenage hooker–dope-addicts you read about, so I went and stood by the gas pumps for a couple of minutes, holding my pack daintily in front of me, with my nose up to the moon like I was trying to Eskimo-kiss its big round face— in other words, trying to make it seem like any minute I expected my nice aunt and uncle to come driving up in their pickup truck and say, Honey, we got lost on the way. How are you, dear?

So he wouldn't worry—I hate to have other people worry about me.

Actually the whole time I was saying under my breath, You wit-nit, you boid brain—not because I was standing there, but because, instead of taking my own advice and hitchhiking to Idaho where I could safely hide out in the Sawtooth Mountains, I had come to the most predictable place in the country, Wahaneeka, Michigan, population 17,000. My place of birth, in other words.

Did that mean I secretly wanted them to track me down?

Yuk, if there's one thing I hate more than yellow cat puke, it's when Dr. Smilax and Associates start saying everyone always has to have a secret motive for everything. Even if it's true, it makes you want to get a bag of natural potato chips and all your Narnia books and go sit under the dining room table for about ten years.

I mean, a part of you always knows what you're doing and why, doesn't it? So you don't always have to pay a million dollars an hour to Peter Smilax, Ph.D., who has so many secret motives of his own, as he looks at you sideways through his inch-thick glasses, that you want to calmly reach over and yank his beard off.

I was standing there, getting madder by the minute at all the headshrinkers I've ever had to deal with. (I have these outbursts regularly, and they're very refreshing. They always make me feel more sure of myself.)

And then, when I saw that the boy in the booth had gone back to reading his magazine, I casually started walking up Main Street (actual name, swear to God), but all the stores and everything were closed, so that it seemed like not just my dad, but everybody else in town, had gone off to Vietnam and gotten killed.

I don't know if I'll ever get to tell Father Jude any of this, but at least I want to write it down while it's still fresh in my mind.

There was one place open, Fisherman's Lounge according to the neon sign in the window. At first I thought it was a bar, only there were lots of families with kids inside, so probably anybody could go in. But just to be on the safe side, I bit my lips to make it look like I was wearing makeup and lifted my chin in the air—stuff my friend Jenny and I used to do when we wanted to act grown-up— and pushed the door open so self-assertively that it banged against the back of somebody's chair inside. Nobody noticed, though, because of all the small-town commotion, or, if they did, at least they had the manners not to stare.

Inside it was freezing cold from the air conditioner, so I had to fish both my sweatshirt and my jacket out of my pack, and while I was at it, this notebook and pen—which was embarrassing since the stuff I was looking for was on the bottom and I had to kneel on the floor to find it all.

Then I sat down at the bar and ordered the Tuesday special, which was all the stew—not fish, thank God—you can eat for $6.95. And while I was waiting, I opened up this notebook so I could take notes for future reference about what it feels like to be back where I was born. Only it felt weird to be writing, so I drew caricatures of the other customers instead.

Later, when I was using my spoon to get up the last of the stew juices, the waitress asked me if I wanted some more, and I nodded my head up and down really hard. So I got to have two plates of it—they serve it on plates here, over noodles—but if you want to know the truth, I could easily have eaten five plates. Or ten plates. But unfortunately she didn't ask again.

I was practicing a speech about how delicious it tasted, etc., etc.—the sort of thing my mom always says in restaurants. Like, What was that herb the chef used, tarragon? You don't suppose we could have an encore? While I look on in horror and admiration.

But when the waitress with her hair in a net slapped the bill on the counter in front of me, I chickened out and left a $2 tip. I'm brave about a lot of things, but not about waitresses unfortunately.

As I was eating, I kept sort of nonchalantly twirling my

bar stool around, holding my milk up like it was a glass of beer, and peering at the inhabitants of the town, who would have been my neighbors if I had grown up here like I was supposed to. I thought about clearing my throat and saying, Could I have everybody's attention for a minute, please? Hi. I'm E. Some of you knew my dad, Richard? The one who was tragically killed in the Vietnam War? Well, I have good news. . . .

The story I told Father Jude.

I always have urges to say things like that at inappropriate times, like during school assembly or when you're supposed to be bowing your head in prayer.

The stew made me sleepy—which must be where the expression "stewed" comes from. I paid and went back outside. After being in the air-conditioned restaurant, I felt like the heat was going to literally knock me off my feet. So I took off my jacket and tied it around my waist and started making plans about where I could realistically spend the night, since I didn't expect to find our house until tomorrow at the earliest.

On the way into town I'd seen a motel called The Little Wigwam, but I didn't want to spend my last fifty bucks on another rickety bed that smelled like people had been you-know-what under the covers.

It was warm out. I figured all I really needed was a secluded place where no bugs or snakes could crawl up my pant legs by mistake. Tomorrow morning I would wake up feeling refreshed, have a bagel for breakfast, and go for a swim in the town pool.

Then I could start looking for my parents' house.

Or better yet, if there were no dykes hanging around in the locker room, like there sometimes are, I could take at least an hour-long shower and wash my hair.

This thought gave me enormous hope. I could take a shower with my clothes on and save having to go to the Laundromat. I did that before, once, when we were on a trip to the Poconos. You get in the shower with everything on except, of course, your shoes and start lathering yourself all over, especially in the pits and crotch. And then after you've flopped around like a clown for about five minutes, you start taking off your clothes, piece by piece, like you're doing a striptease. And then when you're bare naked, you jump up and down on the soggy mass until the water that oozes out isn't gray anymore. The last step is to rinse thoroughly, holding everything up, piece by piece, in the shower spray.

I'd keep just my sundress dry to put on afterwards, bunch everything else up, and when no one was looking, make a dash for it, out the door, down the street. I'd keep running until I came to a farm where I could hang everything up on the branches of a cherry tree.

Then in the afternoon, when I was all sparkling clean, my hair brushed, for a change, I could go into some of the stores on Main Street and say I was my father's daughter. And people would know who I was and be glad to see me, probably, and offer to drive me to our old house.

(Except in my heart of hearts I knew I couldn't really go into any of the stores and say who I was because some well-meaning cow in a calico dress would call my grandmother in Detroit, and she in turn would call my mom. And I would have to be on my way to Idaho again.)

I was walking along, just trusting my instincts about which way to go, which is a mistake I often make, and without really noticing it I came to the end of the residential part of town and passed what must have been an abandoned ice-cream factory, since it had about a five-foot-tall rusty sign in the shape of an ice-cream cone. Pieces of the sidewalk were piled up in the middle, and grass was growing in the cracks. And then the sidewalk just stopped, and I was walking in the weeds on the side of the highway.

I passed a billboard advertising Virginia Slims—I distinctly remember this because I tore a sheet of paper out of this notebook for tinder and started poking around in the debris, hoping to find a used lighter or a book of matches so I could at least *try* to burn the billboard down for encouraging women to get cancer. Once you've gone against Society's norms, you might as well do something worthwhile, for a change.

I've thought about this a lot. My friend Jenny and I, when we were young and idealistic, decided that if either of us ever found out we had leukemia or some other incurable disease, we would at least try to shoot the Ayatollah.

I heard a stereo blasting. Out of nowhere this car came hurtling down the middle of the road, with a bunch of men inside. One of them threw a beer bottle out of the window, which almost hit me—I honestly think that if they had seen me sooner, he would have aimed it at my head. Luckily it only bounced on the ground at my feet and didn't even break. No wonder there's so much trash on the side of the road. There was hysterical laughter, and the car shimmied back and forth, on purpose, like they were mooning me. I stood there and watched them disappear over a rise in the road.

Then, like in a bad dream where you know what's going to happen beforehand, I heard the brakes screech. The light from their headlights as they were backing around looked like a movie that had escaped from the local theater and was running wild in the trees.

The billboard had this ladder thing in back, but at the last minute I ditched my pack and ran across the highway and got down on the ground. I started rolling, with my notebook clutched to my chest, until I came to a stop in a ditch that had something wet in it that smelled like gas or oil. I lay on my side in the fetal position and stared at all the stars in the sky.

I wished my heart would be quiet, but it wouldn't. Not breathing didn't help, either.

The car drove right by me, slowly, stopped about fifty yards down the road, then backed up at at least sixty miles an hour, zigzagging back and forth, and I knew they were going to lose control, skid off the pavement, and roll right over me. But at the last minute they crossed to the shoulder on the other side, and one of them cried, She was right about here! The doors flew open and everybody got out. They were men, not boys. They were all wearing baseball caps. They started going to the bathroom right on the asphalt without being subtle about it or turning their backs.

Their radio was blaring rock-and-roll music from the late 50s, but still I could hear most of what they said. I think they were drunk because the slightest thing made them laugh. They kept saying things for my benefit that I won't repeat. Every other word began with *F.*

That's a dangerous weapon, Devries. Watch where you're pointing it. You can't shoot straight, no way—har, har.

Where'd she go to? Here, pussy, pussy, pussy. Want some nice milk? Guaranteed—ho, ho, ho—fresh.

Here, little hitchhiker. We just stopped to give you a ride, honey—hee, hee, hee!

84

They started saying what they were going to do to me when they found me, all of it too stupid and sickening for words, and I think they were just trying to scare me, but you never know when drunk people are in groups. I decided to stay right where I was and play dead until I saw the shadows of their ugly faces leaning over me. Then I would jump up and make a run for it, right out into the middle of the highway. If another car happened to be coming along, I would run straight at it, waving my arms and screaming. I would dive onto the hood, if necessary, so that they would have to stop and help me.

I'm a pretty fast runner, but if they did catch me and try to do any of the stuff they said, I would bite them wherever I could, just close my eyes and bury my teeth in them until I had one of their fat fingers or whatever in my mouth, and then I would chew it so they'd never be able to sew it back on again. And spit the pieces back into their ugly faces.

I also know how to make myself puke at will.

Even now I can't remember whether you're officially supposed to struggle or not. We talked about this stuff at school, but I can't remember what conclusion, if any, we came to, since Ms. Plover, who was also my Sex and Human Values teacher, just let people talk without ever telling us what she or any other adult thinks, so our class always ended up being just another bull session where the people with the smallest brains and biggest mouths said things that made a normal person not want to eat their lunch.

I was going to struggle. What do you call it in a war when one of the peasants doesn't care whether he dies or not, as long as he takes you down with him? I already had my teeth clenched on one of their imaginary ears.

Then something really sad happened, which considering that they were talking about dragging me into a nearby field and taking turns attacking me, I should probably be thankful for. But one of them found my backpack, where I left it in the bushes, and started pulling stuff out and holding it up and saying things like, Spanky Pants. Here, Mike, that's more your speed. A present, pal.

Suddenly I was so mad the earth began to shake. I wanted to stand up and start shouting things at them. Scratch their eyes out and kick them in the balls.

Then another car drove up and stopped, but unfortunately they were friends of the first car. I heard at least one woman's voice—she kept shrieking with laughter. Out of the corner of my eye I saw the top part of her emerge through the window with a bottle of beer in her hand. She shouted, Mikie's such a faggot, he— I don't even want to write the rest, because it involved doing something to a dead dog, and I happen to love dogs.

Even though it wasn't even remotely funny, she laughed so hard that beer came spewing out of her mouth, all over the side of the car.

The driver calmly called her a stupid bitch.

Every time anyone said anything like that or let out a burp, there was an outburst of laughter, which I took advantage of to squirm and wriggle on my side a few inches. I figured if I could get behind some bushes, I'd at least be in shadow, and then I could get up on all fours and start crawling across the field.

But before I'd squirmed and wriggled more than a yard or so, one of the men said something about breaking somebody's ass, and that got them all revved up again. The drivers got back in their cars and started racing their engines.

Both cars were spraying gravel before all the doors were even shut. At the last minute, as they were squealing onto the highway and starting to drag race each other back to town, a different woman leaned out of the window and shouted, Losers, weepers, honey!

Even after their taillights had disappeared around the bend, the sound of their motors traveled across the fields to where I was hugging myself. Way in the distance, you could hear the music throb. There were faint bursts of laughter.

I remember staring at the sky the whole time. Always before when people tried to get me to see the Big Bear or whatever you call it, all I could see was just a lot of stars, but this time there was this distinct figure in a tunic looming over me.

Then the crickets resumed their chirping, so I sat up. There was muck all over me. Some of it had even gotten into my mouth. I spit about a hundred times but couldn't get rid of the taste.

At first I couldn't take in that they had really stolen my pack. Besides my clothes and stuff like the book I'm supposed to be reading for school, it had my dad's last letter to my mom, which I'd borrowed from her desk sort of as a good-luck charm.

I never should have taken it.

I got up and started walking along the side of the road, kicking the heads off all the dandelions, checking under bushes in the hope that they had flung it out the window without my knowing it.

I wished I had a bow and arrow to shoot them with.

Then I heard a car coming, and I was afraid I was going to go in my pants.

There was a farmhouse with lights on about a quarter of a mile away. I got over the fence as best I could in my condition and started trotting across the open field, twisting my ankle on this stupid clump of dirt so that it still hurts when I press down on it.

The house, as I was running up to it, seemed like my salvation, even though it wasn't on a hill. It had one of those wide porches with a wooden railing that goes halfway around, the sort of house I've always wished we lived in but Mom says we can't afford.

I ran right up the steps without stopping, opened the screen door, and started banging on the knocker with all my might. I rang the bell about twenty times.

I couldn't stop making bleating sounds, like I was a goat or something. I kept looking over both shoulders. When I said, H-help, in a not-very-loud voice, the crickets grew quiet for a few seconds and then started chirping louder than ever.

I rang one more time, then went and sat on the stoop. Somebody definitely lived here. I could wait until they got home and throw myself on their mercy. If they'd let me have a bath and sleep on their couch—or their floor even—I would gladly do the chores in the morning. While I was sitting there, trying to decide what to do, the moon peeked over the roof of the porch, like it was looking for me, and starting shining in my face again.

That made me laugh. I think I was on the verge of hysterics. I remember trying to control my breathing because, if I got an asthma attack now, it was all over. My pills were in my purse, which was in my pack, along with everything else.

It was also dawning on me that I didn't have any more

money, except for what was in my pockets, about $3 in change.

To get my mind on something else, I went and looked in all the windows. Whoever lived there sure had a lot of books! They had walls of books from the floor to the ceiling. I rang the bell hard one more time and listened, but then, on top of everything else, I had to go to the bathroom. Bad. It was an emergency!

I ran around the side of the house and behind a tree, wondering if I could have possibly stumbled onto Aleksandr Solzhenitsyn's house. He's supposed to be holed up in an out-of-the-way place like this. He would have lots of books.

Or J. D. Salinger's—I wished like anything it was J. D. Salinger's house. In my mind I immediately started telling him how my dad had escaped from a VA hospital, and would he mind if we took a bath in his bathtub? That would gain his confidence, because a person isn't going to take a bath in your bathtub and then rob you blind.

I also thought about telling him the stuff I wanted to tell Father Jude and couldn't because I was afraid he would lose respect for me. But judging from J. D. Salinger's stories, he wouldn't be that grossed out.

And maybe after I'd confessed to him, *he*'d trust me enough to explain why he retired from the world when so many people needed him. And maybe, just maybe, I could persuade him to come out of hiding and publish all the books Ms. Plover says he has hidden in his safe. Then I'd get to go on talk shows and act modest and say, Oh, it was nothing, I just tried to be myself and told him the first thing that came into my head.

A car drove sedately past. Its stereo wasn't blaring.

But it also didn't turn in the drive.

Whoever lived here wasn't coming home tonight. I thought about breaking in, just long enough to clean up, but I didn't want to make that mistake again, have the Twemlows come home and go ape-shit.

I stood up and walked sadly away from the road—past the barn, across the field, in the opposite direction to everything. From now on there was nothing holding me back—sort of how it would be if anything ever happened to my mom, which I hope it doesn't.

I could go anywhere I wanted now. Do anything. Shoplift if necessary. Let men go to bed with me and make thousands of dollars.

I didn't have to be nice to people anymore.

I headed across the shadowy fields with the summer sky all around and the moon lighting my way, and when I came to the woods, I wasn't in the least bit afraid—I just kept right on going, using a stick I picked up to keep the spiderwebs out of my face.

I walked for about five or ten miles, it felt like, and eventually I came to the railroad tracks, shining on the ground, and tried walking on the rails, holding my notebook out at the side for balance.

I managed to stay on for a pretty long way, and when the tracks divided, I followed the set that led to a car dump, which is a pretty sad phenomenon, when you stop and think about it—all the people who must have gotten smashed up. But for some reason it looked pretty at night in an eerie sort of way, the hoods of the cars glazed by moonlight.

I was singing.

I have to admit that for a second my heart stopped beating when I saw a dark 50s-model Chevrolet, only it turned out to be a different make, a Pontiac, I think. I opened the back door and climbed right in, made a pillow out of my jacket, and went to sleep.

But only for a few minutes. Outside there was something moving. I quick ducked down to where you put your feet, and started counting one thousand and one, one thousand and two, etc., until I got to one thousand and a hundred, which is a very long time to stay cooped up in one position.

Then very slowly I raised my head and looked around.

It was probably just a skunk or something.

My mind was racing. I started thinking about all the reasons grown-ups do mean things to kids, like maybe their fathers got drunk and took it out on their mothers right before their eyes or kidded them in a rough way that made them insecure about their manhood, and now they were just getting back at Society.

It sort of helps to psychoanalyze people who are mean to you.

But then, what always happens when I do that, I started thinking of other things that were bothering me, other people who've screwed me one way or another. And the next thing I knew, I was going through all the names on my shit list, checking them off one by one.

Because, to tell you the truth, the way one of the men had been standing, with his shoulders kind of hunched over when he was taking a leak, reminded me exactly of Barry Comstock, my former stepfather. Of the way he stands when he's coaching soccer. And all of a sudden, Barry was the person I was mad at. The person I wished something bad would happen to.

I'm sitting there in an abandoned car, my chin resting on the back of the front seat, thinking, What a careless man. Because, literally, he could care less.

I know I must sound like I'm demented, but I was thinking of going back and tying a wire cable around the bottom of the billboard, and then running to the other side of the road and waiting until I heard their stereo getting louder, and then calmly raising it to exactly the height of the windshield and carefully wrapping it as many times as I could around the nearest tree so that it would break the glass and garrote them.

With Barry somehow in the front seat.

Unfortunately, probably because I watch too much television, I couldn't help seeing a cartoon version of all this, in which the wire drew the car back like an arrow and then, when it was taut and the whole state of Michigan was straining with the pull, fired it halfway across the continent until it fell on the desert floor somewhere Out West in Idaho, which seemed pretty tame, since in the cartoons people always crawl out of accidents like that without any lasting wounds.

I had to re-imagine the scene, this time tying a brick or an old piece of machinery like I'd seen on the side of the road in just the right place. So that it would smash the windshield right in front of their ugly faces.

And this time, instead of a cartoon, I saw a horror movie of their grisly deaths and, in a closeup, Barry's eyes like two fried eggs.

My real father was always very gentle with children and animals, my mom said once. Dad, I said out loud. Where are you?

I was panting. I was staring out the window, watching

for any sign of movement. If I really did put up a wire, and the driver really did lose control and smash into the side of the road, then a tow truck would eventually have to tow the car out here. Once I thought that, there was no way I could stop from seeing a bunch of dead bodies crowded in the backseat of the car next to me, which, now that I looked closely, kind of resembled the car of the men who were bothering me.

Needless to say, I started imagining them coming to life and quietly getting out of their car all hunched over, stumbling in my direction, with their soft zombie arms open wide. I went to put my hand down, and there was this big glob of fungus on the seat—actually it was just some stuffing coming out of the upholstery. But before I realized that, I had kicked the door open, scrambled out, and was about half a mile away, trotting through the bracken.

There was less and less point in trying to sleep.

I decided to just stay up and walk around outdoors until the sun came up and it was daylight out. Then I could always go to the town park, where it had to be safe to sit on one of the benches and catnap unless some bum with his zipper unzipped tried to sit down next to me, which really happened once in Washington.

I started following this stream that I wouldn't have even noticed if it hadn't been making little slippery, slurping sounds. I was wondering what my mom would think if she could see me now. One thing I like about her is she never says, I told you so. But she does get this sad look, which is almost worse.

Watching me in her crystal ball, she would now know that on top of everything else I had swiped Dad's last letter and lost it.

Then I came to a clearing that was so pretty I wished somebody else was there to see it with me. I hate nature descriptions, maybe because I'm not very good at them, and, to tell you the truth, when I come to one in a book, I always skip ahead, but the moon was just pouring its light on everything, and the stream was all quicksilver, and there were trees standing quietly by.

I was a part of it, too.

You know the riddle, If a tree falls over on a desert island, and there's nobody around to hear it, does it make any sound? (The answer is, Trees don't grow on desert islands.) Well, I felt like all this was happening just for me because I was literally the only person there to see it.

So, of course, I starting taking my clothes off, and the first thing I did was rinse my shirt and my underwear out as best I could and hang them up to dry on a pine tree. Then I stepped into the water up to my shins, and even though the water felt cool at first, it was incredibly refreshing, and I made myself squat down so I could wash every part of me and get rid of the petroleum smell, among others. I used handfuls of water on my front and sides.

After a while you got used to it, and it was what they're always saying on TV commercials—heavenly. Taking a bath outdoors on a warm summer's night, looking up and seeing the same group of stars, which means I'll always be able to find them now—I can't even begin to describe what it was like.

I stayed in the water for a long time, picking up stones that glowed on the bottom. What's really amazing is that along the bank, where the current is slower, the stream is like a dark mirror, so that when you put your hand in the water to make the stars shiver, you sort of see a movie of yourself.

And maybe because it was the middle of the night and I just happen to look my best in the dark, for once I actually thought I wasn't that bad looking. I looked female. I looked like a nude in a book of photographs.

And as I stood there admiring myself and gently massaging my poor tummy—I noticed, by the way, that my belly button, which for 15 and 5/6 years has been an inny, is now an outy—I got to thinking that except for maybe the way my hair is cut and the fact that my teeth are straight, there is nothing to mark me as a girl of the 80s.

You couldn't prove just by looking at me that I wasn't somebody from the Past who had just woken up from her thousand years' nap and decided to take a bath. And here she was, reincarnated, with her hairy parts dripping—*if* you can think of people back then as having hairy parts, since the most they ever show in paintings is just a dab of pink. I can, but then my mind's in the gutter half the time, anyway.

I don't know why I found this idea so reassuring, except that it made me feel immortal, like I was part of an endless chain of mother-daughter-mother-daughter, stretching back to the Dawn of Man. Like my womb was a time machine.

And while I was having these profound thoughts, I heard a far-off tinkling sound. Without stopping to think, I went leaping over to where my pants were lying on the ground, danced right into them—I could have cared less that the backs of my legs were still wet. Threw on my still-damp shirt. Plucked my socks and undies off the tree and stuffed them in my pocket. I didn't even take time to tie my sneakers.

This is probably the first irrefutable proof that I'm kabadocuckoo, but even though it was after midnight, all I could think was, The Ice Cream Man is coming! I started going in every direction at once, trying to figure out where the tinkling was coming from. In my mind's eye I could just see him on his ice cream cycle, driving up a moonlit road, his bell sort of absentmindedly tinkling in the breeze.

I already knew what I would get: a toasted—pant, pant—toasted almond, please!

And at the sound of my voice coming from the woods, he would of course drive into a ditch, and I would have to go and help him to his feet. I wanted him to be a nice college boy like the one who really did use to drive his Good Humor cycle down our street in New Hampshire. His name was Stan Jolly.

I'd go, Please, Mom? Please?

Stan would drive by our house *v e r y   s l o w l y,* knowing that at the last minute my mom would say, Oh, all right. She would press the pause button on the VCR, where she spends hours going over the same documentary, and get up to find her purse.

When he saw me coming, he'd coast to a stop, swing his long legs over the whatever-you-call-it—saddle—and trot around to the side where they keep the ice cream. Pull on the magic silver handle. And a wisp of vapor would waft out into the evening air. . . . I was so homesick for the good old days, before everything in my life got messed up.

For just last summer, in other words, and all the summers before.

Jenny's mom would always give her money, too, and afterwards we would go sit on the curb, trying to make our ice creams last forever, and if Barry was out watering the lawn, he'd let some of the water run down the driveway so we could race our sticks in the gutter.

Of course, I knew in my heart of hearts that it would have been a stupid thing to do, spend the last of my money on ice cream. If there really had been an ice cream man and not just another phantom of my diseased imagination.

But sometimes not doing something because it's stupid or whatever doesn't even seem like a consideration.

I stood balancing on a wooden fence, trying to decide which way to jump, because sometimes the sound got louder and sometimes it seemed almost to disappear. Across the road was a driveway overgrown with bushes that led up the side of a hill. An old rusty sign said NO TRESPASSING.

I got down from the fence and crossed the road.

You know how when you're coming home from school, not paying any attention to where you're going, it's not that big a deal when your feet automatically turn up your own drive?

I kid you not: my feet started walking right up the driveway.

There was a gray rabbit meditating under a berry bush who wasn't the least bit scared when I walked up to him— he raised himself up on his hoppers and sniffed the moon and then just flopped away. And a little farther on was the gate my mother used to tell me about when I was little, because I used to always ask her questions about how she met my dad and where they lived, etc., etc., only it was a lot more rickety than I had imagined.

The latch was so rusted shut that I had to whack it with a rock. When I finally got it open and started pushing it in front of me, it made a moaning sound, as if to say, What took you so long?

You can't see the house itself until you walk halfway around the curve, but it's there, right on top of the hill like

Mom said, without any bushes or anything for transition. And hanging from the ceiling of the half-tumbled-down porch was this old dinner bell, moving slightly every time there was a breeze, sending a lazy tinkling sound out into the universe.

The yard was all crisscrossed with giant tire tracks like some asshole had been driving his tractor back and forth across our lawn. I stood with my back to the house and could see for miles, not because it's that big of a hill, but because everything else around here is so flat.

Then I walked around the house, pounding on all the boards until this old-fashioned key dropped out from behind one of them that was loose. It took some twisting and turning to get the kitchen door open. To be on the safe side, I said, Excuse me! Anybody home? in a fairly loud voice.

But of course nobody was.

The furniture had all been covered up. What there was, was pretty old and decrepit. Which isn't surprising, since the house has remained unoccupied for sixteen years, except for every fall when my Uncle Jimmy and his buddies come up here to quote unquote hunt deer, though according to my mom the only time they ever came back with anything was when one of them hit a doe or a fawn by mistake and totaled his car. Mom wishes my grandmother would sell the place, because of unhappy associations, but the market is depressed.

I don't know whether you're going to believe this or not, but the moment I stepped inside, even though I've never actually been here before (except as a fetus), I immediately recognized our family smell, sort of a cross between stale dough and a fire that's gone out.

Unborn children are a lot more aware of their environments than people realize, and someday they're going to discover that half of what a person is like when they grow up is influenced by the things that happened around them when they were still in the womb.

For example, I knew exactly where everything would be. In the entryway there were stacks of newspapers and magazines, so I grabbed a couple and started upstairs to use the john, which has little stars painted on the ceiling, but in the nick of time I thought, Yipes! What if the flusher doesn't work! So I went back outside and around the house to a field where I think there are sugar beets growing—do they have sugar beets in Michigan? Whatever they are, I cleaned one off with spit and tried it, while I was squatting in the rows, and they're not the greatest-tasting things in the world, but they don't kill you. I figure if it's a vegetable growing in a field, it must be good for you, but I always start with just a small bite to make sure I don't die or anything.

Anyway, you realize what this means??? It means Effie is going to be okay. She's not going to starve to death.

I went back inside and explored as best as I could in the light coming in the windows. Unfortunately I didn't find any old letters or photographs or family heirlooms worth a fortune. They just had the sort of junk you'd find in anybody's house.

From the attic window you can see practically forever in both directions, fields and forests, here and there the pale face of another old farmhouse. One of them is supposed to belong to the Trowbridges, my Dad's foster parents, so therefore sort of my grandparents. My mom says they may or may not still be alive. In a day or two, when I feel more settled, I may go over and introduce myself.

I went back downstairs and carefully took the sheet off

one of the armchairs—I'm allergic to dust mites, and the last thing I wanted was to raise a cloud of dust. Then I sat down for a few minutes to relax, and the next thing I knew I was sound asleep.

In fact, I must have slept for a couple of hours because when I woke up it was starting to get less dark out. Somewhere there were birds twittering. The waning moon or whatever-you-call-it was almost gone. First I became aware that a faint gray light was shining on my face, so I turned sleepily sort of upside down, which is how I like to sleep in a comfortable chair, and buried my face deep in the cushion.

Then, when I finally realized that the phone was ringing, I said, Barry, could you get that, please? because in my dream I was cooking his supper.

He didn't hear me, of course, because he wasn't there.

I opened my eyes a crack, saw there really was a phone, and vaguely wished it would stop ringing. It didn't penetrate at first that there shouldn't be a working phone in a supposedly abandoned house. All I wanted was to go back to sleep.

But the ringing didn't stop. Only after I don't know how long did it finally get through my petrified skull that whoever was on the other end had to know I was there, because they didn't just let it ring six or seven times, the way you do on the off-chance they're in the john or something. It rang at least fifty times. I know because by this time I was wide awake and counting. I still have marks on my arms from where I hugged myself. I just knew it was the people who took my pack since it had my dad's last letter with *this address* on it!

Finally I couldn't stand it anymore. I reached over and

lifted the receiver up a fraction of an inch, just enough to make the ringing stop.

Very cautiously I put the receiver to my ear, but whoever it was, was waiting for me to go first, because there was no hello or anything on the other end.

All I could hear, if I listened very closely, was something that sounded like the wind blowing. Or very soft breathing. I took a chance and whispered, "Dad?" and he tapped three times.

I started laughing so hard that the tears trickled down my temples and into my hair. I cried, "I should have known it would be you! Dad, how are you? Are you okay?"

Three more taps, but faint ones like he was calling long distance from very far away.

"How'd you track me down?" I asked. "Never mind, you can tell me later. I *knew* this was where I should go. Aren't I smart? I mean, where else would we go to find each other? Should I wait for you here, or do you want me to come where you are? Where are you, by the way? The only thing is, I can't go home. I'll explain why when I see you, and then you'll understand.

"Dad," I said, "are you there?"

I could hear cars whizzing by.

"Dad?" I said. "I've been doing a lot of thinking. I just figured out the truth about you: that you've been here all along. I don't know why it's taken me so long, duh. I mean, you did get shot in the war, etc., etc., but they found you *a long time ago*, back when I was just a baby and the war was still going on, and shipped you home in a big jet.

"And for a couple of weeks you really did stay in the

army hospital at Valley Forge, but then they transferred you to a facility for the permanently disabled in Florida, because, to be perfectly candid, they thought you were a vegetable.

"For personal reasons, which I understand but can't condone, you must have thought that with your terrible wounds you'd be inflicting yourself on Mom and me, so you decided to play dead. So for sixteen long years, which is a whole lifetime to some of us, you never said *a word*, never let on by expression or deed that you were as much a sentient human being as the rest of us. They had no way of knowing who that hunk of flesh with the protruding ears was, much less that there was a functioning brain in there.

"Which is why, by the way, they never bothered to fix your face—what does a vegetable need a face for? Only, according to Father Jude, if you will admit to being a person, if you will only show other people the side of yourself you've shown me, you will of course be eligible to get a new face. We'll ask them to give you a James Dean face, and then you can be in the movies and get rich and famous—ha ha, just kidding. I'm *so* glad you called! To tell you the truth, I was beginning to get a little worried. Dad?"

There were no taps. I listened as hard as I could. It occurred to me it might be a trap, but it was worth the risk.

"You know what else I've realized?" I said. "Well, maybe it's conceited of me, but half the time I have this feeling that I can read your mind. Like you're probably wondering if you did the right thing in getting in touch with me in the first place. You did, I promise you. I've grown up an incredible amount in the last few days, a lot of it thanks to you. It embarrasses me to think how childishly I acted before. I still have a long way to go, but in terms of maturity I'm already at least five years older."

Pause. No response.

Something told me it was now or never. That I had to keep talking, talk him in out of the cold, so to speak. Have you ever seen the movie *Close Encounters of the Third Kind*? Do you remember how they had to coax the aliens down from the sky? That's exactly how I felt. I had to just keep babbling on in my usual way, as though it was perfectly natural for a father to be standing in a telephone booth on the edge of the highway, listening to his daughter and not even tapping or anything. I never doubted for a second that he could hear me. I just prayed that I was saying the right things.

I said, "In the last few days I've been trying to imagine exactly what it was like, the war and everything. That's the kind of imagination I have. If I can't work something out to the last detail, my mind just quits. The fantasy goes poof. Do you know what I mean? Like, I could never in a million years imagine doing anything with Mikhail Baryshnikov because I could never work out the steps leading up to it—I've tried to more than once, so I know. In my fantasies I always have to settle for kissing Harvey Whittaker, a boy I met at the pool. He's nice, he's just not Misha."

I laughed. "You want to know what I think happened? There were a lot of casualties on the road from Hanoi, but somehow, despite your grievous wounds, you managed to drag yourself over to the nearest body, someone more or less your size, and when you'd made sure he wasn't breathing, that his skin felt like an old pumpkin, you switched dog tags with him. Duh, I guess it didn't take very many brains to figure that out, but as a kid I used to think about this a lot—it was the point where my imagination used to get stuck.

"But now it's perfectly clear. They put *his* body in *your* grave and sent Mom *your* dog tags, which to this day she keeps in the same drawer as her jewelry and panty hose. And after they shipped you home to the hospital, the other guy's poor widow came to see you probably. And knowing you, you just lay there like a zombie, waiting to see what would happen. Which was that after two or three visits, she decided it was hopeless and filed for divorce. And you, being of little faith, thought Mom would do the same thing."

I took a deep breath. "Dad," I said, trying to be as patient as I could—I knew this was hard for him. "It's important for us to get back together. We need each other. But you've got to help. You can't expect me to do everything."

Then I told him about you, Father, about how you were the one person I trusted, and that if we went to see you together, you would try to help us, with no strings attached. I talked and talked, for a really long time, for at least half an hour, it felt like, and the whole time he said nothing, *nothing*, I mean, NOTHING, like he really was dead and had called me up from the Afterlife. For a second I wondered if I really wanted him to come back—what if he was all mutilated like in that story about the monkey's paw?

I got this cold feeling, something made me turn around—the doorknob was moving. I screamed. I stood there with the phone in my hand, screaming like a girl in a horror movie. And he came in, in his old uniform, going shh with his finger, and for a second he didn't look like he had before, like someone who'd gotten their face blown off in the war. He looked like a nice boy, my age. It must have been the light.

When he came closer to take the phone out of my hand, I recognized him from the picture my mom keeps on her dresser. At first I couldn't think of anything to say—what can you say in a situation like that? I went up to him, I put my arms around him, and—don't laugh, please—we started dancing. There was no music or anything—we just danced to the sound of our own footsteps. *Clop, clop, clop.*

But then I started thinking that somebody should tell him, that it wasn't fair not to, so as gently as I could, I said, "Uh, Dad, there's this rumor going around that you're dead."

He leaned away from me and, in the first light of day, I saw that his eyes were laughing. And in a whisper, softer than a person breathing, he said, "Well, I'm not, am I?"

T
he
pathe
tic tru
th abou
t   E. B.:
a confe
ssion&&

&

To Whom It May Concern:

I just woke up from another dream about Barry Comstock. This time I dreamt it was last spring and we were staying with Les(s) Smith at his summer house on Cape Cod, which Mom and I really did for about three weeks while our stuff was being sent by truck from New Hampshire to Virginia.

I was going around knowing full well I had screwed up everyone's life, including my own, and feeling like I couldn't breathe, almost. I was desperate for an excuse to get out of the house, so in my dream I shouted upstairs that I'd take her skirt to the cleaners. And from somewhere startlingly close, Mom goes, Why, thank you, precious!

Then I ran—away from the voice and, although it's not

physically possible, all the way back to the house we used to live in, in New Hampshire. One minute I was banging on the kitchen door and the next, without any transition, I was upstairs in Barry's arms, telling him everything I wasn't able to the last time we met. And he kept gobbling up my tears, going, shh, don't worry, everything's going to be all right, plucking the buttons off the front of my shirt.

I remember saying, I thought you were tired of me. His face was rough, and he kept rubbing it hard against mine, huffing and puffing. Finally he gasped, I could do this all night.

That's when I woke up.

Usually I only let myself think about him when I'm out walking—that way it doesn't hurt as much. But you can't make yourself not dream about someone, can you?

I know I shouldn't be writing any of this down, but who the hell is ever going to see it? Afterwards I can rip out the pages and tear them up and chew the pieces until they're a soggy mess and then spit them out in different places in the woods or maybe even swallow them.

Shit, fuck, damn, piss. I don't care whether it's good for me or not. JUST THIS ONCE I'M GOING TO WRITE *EVERYTHING* DOWN!!!

(I better start a new page.)

&&

I don't know where to start. Yes, I do, with the night Mom went to her Women's Support meeting and at supper beforehand I asked Barry if he'd be willing to read my story for English. He glanced at Mom, then smiled at me and started nodding his head up and down really hard, as if to say, There's nothing in the world I'd rather do. Mom had to go get ready, so he went and took a shower because he had just come back from lacrosse. He was singing the aria from *La Bohème* that he always sings in the shower, and Mom and I started howling like coyotes.

Then he came out with just a towel on and his hair combed back, which always makes his head look grotesquely small, and he said to Mom, You still here? (So I guess he didn't hear us howling, after all.) And Mom said, I really don't feel like going. He just smiled and shrugged his shoulders. I don't blame you, he said. Last time you all sat around trying to decide if Peggy Lapchick should have a baby or not. (Peggy Lapchick can't decide whether to have a baby or not. She teaches history and is a Lesbian.)

Mom made her don't-be-such-a-male-chauvinist-pig face. I should go, she said, because Jane will be there. She feels as strongly about the spouses-in-the-faculty-locker-room issue as we do. (Jane Smaller is the headmaster's wife. The women teachers don't like the spouses using their locker room. Mom was on the spouses' side, but she hates it when women start fighting other women.)

My dad said, Oh, and went upstairs.

I said, Don't go, Mom. But she just patted my hand and said, If you believe in something, you have to stick up for it, even if you'd rather stay home where it's warm.

She heaved herself out of the hall chair and went and got her coat. It was February 19. There had been a big snow-storm the day before. I can still see her using both hands and feet to climb over the hill of snow the snowplow had left between the front of our house and the street.

After she left, B. built a fire in the fireplace, and when I said, Are you expecting a student? he looked sort of sur-prised and said, I thought I was supposed to read your story. Duh, I said, and went and got it for him.

I remember sitting on my bed, staring at my algebra book and wondering what my story would sound like to someone who was reading it for the first time—especially to him, since all the students say he's the best critic in the whole English department.

After about fifteen minutes he called me from the bot-tom of the stairs. E., come down here. (He always called me E.) I sort of bounced down. I remember everything I had on: my Timberland boots, my white corduroys, my purple turtleneck, the wooden thing I got in Bar Harbor to hold my hair back.

He was sitting on the floor in the living room, smoking his pipe. He looked exactly like how I imagine the hero of a Harlequin Romance looks, though I hasten to add that I've only read one, purely out of curiosity, and it nearly made me puke.

My story was spread out in front of him. He patted the floor beside him, so I sat down Indian style and hugged my knees and stared at the fire. Then he started telling me that, considering my age, I was some kind of literary genius, that I would probably turn out to be one of the spokespersons for my generation, and other stuff I don't have to write down because I'll never forget it. The main thing was he liked it.

He said my mom wouldn't approve of him telling me this—apparently they had even discussed it. *He* thought they should, because if you have talent, you shouldn't keep it under a bushel, which is one of his favorite sayings. But I guess my mom was afraid that it would go to my head and I would start writing novels when I should be studying algebra and biology (my two worst subjects), that my grade point would suffer, and I would end up at the University of New Hampshire—which is actually a pretty place (I've been there). It's just not Harvard, Princeton, or Yale.

Anyway, I wasn't supposed to tell her that he'd told me, so of course I said I wouldn't.

He didn't say much about the story itself, except that parts of it were childish, parts incredibly mature. I just sat there, looking at the fire. He said the main character kept going back and forth between being a girl and a woman, but that was the beauty of her.

Then he pushed the hair out of my eyes. Are you listening? I said yes. He turned my chin like I was a model or something and started saying I had unique coloring because my eyes are blue-gray and my hair's almost black. He said I had a Wheaties-and-cream complexion. At first I was confused, because I couldn't see what any of this had to do with my story, though, needless to say, I liked hearing that he thought I was pretty.

Actually that's not 100-percent true. Part of me wasn't

confused, but I couldn't believe he was saying what I thought he was. I could feel the fire on my cheeks. He jumped up and poked the wood with the poker, and sparks flew up. My heart was pounding. I remember that I kept taking deep breaths like I'd been running or something.

Then he grabbed my boot and started pulling it off. I said, calmly, like this happened all the time, What are you doing? trying not to laugh.

I want to hold your foot, he said—which he did. He sat back down and nested my foot in his lap. I had on a heavy wool sock at least two days old.

Why are you acting so crazy?

I'm acting crazy? he said.

Maybe I was, too, without realizing it. I would look at him, to see what expression he had on his face, then back at the fire.

My face was sore from grinning so much.

For about five minutes, if you can believe it, we sat there without saying a word. Then he started saying in a low voice that every stepfather and stepdaughter had to work out their own relationship, because there was no pre-scribed one. They couldn't just consult someone else about it.

That's when it definitely clicked, the part before about not telling Mom he had told me I was a writer. This can't be happening, I thought. I looked at him.

I like you in a complicated way, he said. As my daughter, of course, but also as my student, my friend, a stranger, my mother, and my lover, all at once.

Oh, gawd! I thought. I don't understand what you mean, I said.

He said that he was a "feeling type" in the Jungian sense

and never knew himself exactly what he meant, but he always began by being absolutely honest about how he *felt*. Then he would try to figure things out from there.

I didn't know what to say.

He was looking straight at me. You have to help, he said. Our relationship concerns us both—and no one else. He said that, when he talked like this, he was talking to the *woman* in me.

So I said, Why do you think I'm a stranger?

Everyone's a stranger to some extent. He said he felt the same way about my mom. Even more so. How do you feel about me? he asked. Be absolutely honest.

He looked very vulnerable, like it really mattered to him one way or the other, so I said, Like you're my father? My friend? My teacher? I felt like my face was on fire. I guess a stranger, too, I said—because I really do think of other people as strangers, only I always thought before that was just another one of *my* peculiarities.

Is that all? he asked in a muffled voice.

I had to look and see what his expression was because he sounded—like he was going to cry or something. Honest to God, he sounded like a little boy.

I guess, I said.

I think he could see I was embarrassed, because he started laughing. I started laughing, too.

Does this seem crazy, what we're doing?

Not crazy, I said.

Strange?

I nodded vigorously!

Wrong?

I said I didn't know.

He said to him it felt natural. Kneel, he said. I looked at

him like he'd gone kabadocuckoo. In his schoolteacher voice he said, *Kneel!*

So I knelt. He knelt, too, and put his arms around me and hugged me and said, I'm hugging you, E., in all the ways I just said. I said, Even as a stranger? and he said, Even as a lover.

He leaned away from me. He wasn't laughing. He wasn't even smiling. He looked almost sad. Very fetching, as Mom would say. I sort of smiled and sat back down and said, Oh.

He scooted over next to me. I don't have any preconceived ideas, he said. All I know is how I feel—which is that I want to be alone with you like this, from time to time. Well, not exactly like this. And I want us to discover what our relationship is going to be—together.

Does this mean I have to sleep with you? I asked, and he looked like he had just swallowed a turkey bone. Then he burst out laughing. Not necessarily, he said, laughing. It depends. We'll only do what both of us want to do.

I just said, Oh.

He said, How do you feel about my holding your foot? I said, Indifferent. He pretended to be hurt, so I said, Maybe you could stroke my nose instead. I guess he thought I was serious because he started stroking my proboscis. Oh, Barry, yes, that does feel nice, I said, and we both sort of laughed.

When he looked at me like that and we laughed at the same time, I felt like—I don't know how to describe it. Like he and I were in outer space, circling the earth. Needless to say, I was very conscious of being attracted to him. To his hair, especially, for some reason. It had dried in a funny way, and I was dying to reach out and touch one of his curls. But I didn't dare.

116

Somehow it did seem wrong—not wrong, but something told me no one else would ever understand, which is how "wrong" usually feels to me. Especially not my mom, even though once when I was supposedly asleep in the backseat of the car and we were coming back from somewhere, I overheard her say to Barry that she was starting to worry about me because I wasn't more interested in boys. When I was her age, she said, I was already grooving with guys in college. At the time he just laughed. They both laughed.

I don't know what it says about me, but I honestly never stopped to think that I was betraying her. God, that sounds obtuse, but it's true. Maybe because of the rumors I used to hear about him, which neither he nor my mom ever confirmed or denied. It's a long story, but I happen to know personally of at least one time he fooled around with someone else, and I remember thinking at the time, I would be better for him than that slut.

It couldn't be wrong just because he was older than me, since that was only an accident of fate.

To tell you the truth, I don't know what I thought. I thought a hundred things at once, and at the same time I didn't want to think or say anything that would spoil the mood. Besides, how could stroking a person's nose be morally evil? He wasn't my real father. I was old enough. Compared to most teenagers in the United States, I'm sexually retarded.

I kept praying that the feeling of wrongness would go away. Either that, or I would stop feeling so attracted to him so I could go type the final draft of my story, which was due the next morning at 9:30.

Actually, now that I think about it, it's kind of funny.

He was solemnly stroking my nose, which of course made me grin. Then he started touching my mouth, like he was trying to catch my smile or something, which made me laugh. Then he moved closer, sort of got up on his knees, and started touching me everywhere where a person can't really object—on my forehead, on my ears, on my hair, on my throat, on the tips of my fingers.

I felt like I was going to have an asthma attack. My heart was going *boom, boom, boom.* I wondered at the time if he could hear it.

He was busy making little *x*'s on the front of my sweater when the doorbell rang. Shit! he said under his breath. He jumped up and went to the door. I got up, too, thinking it was probably my mom. My face was all red in the mirror. It looked like I'd been drinking. I made faces at myself, flaring my nostrils and sticking my tongue out. Then I went and stood in the doorway of the living room, where I could hear him talking to Mr. Smaller, the headmaster.

I know you got a chick in there, the headmaster was saying in a loud voice. He sounded drunk. Don't tell me you were grading papers. Listen, what's-your-name. Cumstuck. I figured while our wives were out bad-mouthing us, I'd come over and keep you company. Commiserate. Look, I brought you something.

Barry was saying, The truth is, I don't feel so hot—otherwise, I'd ask you in. I think it's just a cold, but every time I turn around I get diarrhea.

There was a silence. It sounded like the headmaster was either sniffing real loud or maybe crying. Maybe he was trying to verify my dad's alibi. Finally I heard him say, Your house is on fire, man. Fire! Fire!

Shh, Barry said. It's okay. It's in the fireplace. Listen, Cholly, why don't you go see if Busang's in. He'd love to have a drink with you.

The headmaster started muttering, Goddamn mathematician. I want to drink with a humanist, not a goddamn mathematician. He made one of his speeches, the humor of which was lost on me.

Barry kept going, Shh!

Finally the headmaster said, Well, here—at least drink the drink. I'm afraid a little of it may have spilled on the way over. It'll help your cold. You have a cold, you know. I can tell. You look all flushed. I have one, too. It's this goddamn weather.

What is it? Barry asked.

I don't know. Let me see. Hmm, smells like gin. That smell like gin to you?

Jesus, Cholly, this is straight gin. How many of these have you had?

Another pause. Then the headmaster said, You know something, Comstock? You're a Puritan. You're like—and he spit the name out like it was the grossest swear—Jonathan Edwards. I bet your wife doesn't have any fun at all. Imagine all that talent wasted on Jonathan Edwards, the Puritan.

By now my dad was sort of laughing, too, though I could tell he wasn't that amused. Mr. Smaller must have started away from our house. I heard him call out, You're too puritanical, Comstock. I'm going over to Busang's house, see if I can screw his wife.

After what seemed like forever, my dad came back in and shut the door. He put his hand on my shoulder and didn't say anything. Then he looked in my eyes like he was trying to read my mind or send me a message or something. I don't know what would have happened next if Mr. Smaller hadn't started kicking, this time at the side door.

Open up! he shouted. Gotta use your can, Edwards! You could hear him laughing his Ernie laugh. My dad didn't move. He just stood there, with his hand on my shoulder, staring in my eyes. Like Mr. Smaller didn't exist.

I thought it was funny. We heard him mutter stuff like, Wait a minute, I don't want to screw Busang's wife. Face like a horse. No tits. I want to screw Comstock's wife. Eat her up. He pounded on the door a couple of times, but with less conviction. Must be on the can himself, he said out loud.

When it had been quiet for about thirty seconds, we tiptoed to the window where we could see him going to the bathroom in the snow. When he was done and he had put himself back together, he carefully picked up his little tray of glasses and walked back down the hill.

Luckily our house was kind of isolated because there are teachers at the school who would *not* have appreciated seeing their headmaster act like that. Usually he's very charming, and everyone thinks he's a nice guy. *I* don't, but I'm always in the minority. I think he acts nice because he wants people to like him. He's always trying to butter the students up. When he sees me on the path, he always says something supposedly witty like, We can't go on meeting like this. His real name is Charles, by the way, but up there they always call him Cholly.

My dad and I went in the kitchen and started doing the dishes, which was a good thing because pretty soon Mom really did come home. Nothing else happened that night.

Nothing happened until Mom went to Boston to film the Pro-Choice demonstration, which was over a week later—ten days, to be exact.

Barry kept leaving joke notes in my student mailbox—"From your secret admirer." Or if we happened to be alone together, like the time we were both jogging in the old gym, he'd wait until no one else was around, and then he'd reach over and stroke my nose. But I was pretty sure that sooner or later we'd end up going to bed together.

Needless to say, my mom and I don't always see eye to eye on Barry. I'm not saying he doesn't have his faults, like any other human being. But he's not a monster or anything. She forgets that once upon a time he could almost always make her laugh. He knows how to surprise people into laughing.

We used to be so happy. The three of us. Mom told me that when they were first engaged, he said he was marrying both of us. And I thought—and still think, sometimes—that he was the best stepfather any girl could ask for. I remember thinking, This one we're going to keep.

They met a long time ago in New York City where they

were both active in the Peace Movement—supposedly they had something to do with getting us out of Vietnam. Back then they were just comrades, since Mom was in the process of marrying her film teacher, Professeur le Weirdo, the one she always says doesn't count—pun intended because he turned out *not* to be a count, his claims to the contrary notwithstanding, plus all his degrees from places like the University of Budapest were completely fake. She was into brains at the time.

This was after my real dad died, but the war was still going on. Barry started out as a conscientious objector, but then a relative high up in the State Department helped him get a 4-F for medical reasons (he had a slight nervous breakdown when he was in college). So he joined the Peace Corps instead. He wasn't required to or anything—he's just very idealistic and always trying to do something to better humanity. He also wanted to get away from his crazy New England family, which was mostly his mother, plus a lot of old aunts. Who wouldn't?

He spent two years in one of those South American countries where they're always having a revolution. Officially he was an English teacher, but in fact he spent most of his time distributing birth control devices—he and my mom are both kind of fanatical about the Population Explosion.

I guess his efforts weren't appreciated by the Catholic church, which is pretty big down there, because the priests were always trying to sabotage his efforts, telling the peasants they would go to hell if they attended his evening classes. Which meant that in a lot of cases the women got the contraceptives, but not the instructions that went with them, so some of the more ignorant ones put them under their mattresses instead of in their vaginas and got pregnant, anyway. As a result, his credibility got somewhat tarnished, and he had to start from square one.

I'll tell you something that happened once, if you promise not to read a lot of garbage into it or submit it as a case study to *Psychology Today*. I was about twelve at the time—i.e., it was so long ago that sometimes I wonder if it really happened or if I just imagined it.

It really happened.

Mom's Hungarian was always returning from long trips and then taking off again. So half the time he wasn't around, which was okay with me—I didn't care about him one way or the other, except that I liked the presents he was always bringing me.

I got a ride home from drama camp with somebody else's mom, so I didn't have to take the bus, and instead of getting back around suppertime, as planned, it was the middle of the afternoon. I remember thinking how surprised she would be.

Since no one answered the door, I used the key on my string necklace to get in. Mom? I said, plopping my pack down on the living room floor. I went into the bedroom. Mom?

That was the first time I met Barry. He was sitting up in bed like a king with a sheet over his lap, going, Shh, your mom's asleep. I'm Barry Comstock—pleased to meet you. We even shook hands.

I was all sweaty and covered with mosquito bites. I remember showing him this humongous one on my arm. He seemed very concerned.

Now of course I can't help wondering what it must have

been like for poor Mom, waking out of a deep sleep to find her latest boyfriend talking to her twelve-year-old daughter who was unexpectedly looming up from the darkness at the foot of the bed.

But at the time all I knew was that I liked him. I had to have felt somewhat embarrassed for invading their privacy and all, for waking them up. And I guess I had some vague idea about what they'd been doing. But Barry was so good at putting himself in other people's shoes that he knew just how to act. He never once made me feel unwelcome.

Mom, however, had a cow pie. She followed me into the bathroom, mixing up the buttons of her bathrobe and saying stuff like, How do you feel, darling? Are you confused? Mr. Comstock is a good friend and needed a place to sleep. And so on and so forth.

I'm not saying that had anything to do with what Barry and I did, but I honestly used to wonder if Mom didn't secretly know what was going on, and for whatever inscrutable adult reasons, not care. Or maybe even think it was—natural. You know, that it would be good for me. I know that sounds terribly naive, but she never once said anything when he acted crazy around me, like nudging me off the pavement when we were out walking or kissing my elbow good-night. She would just look up at the sky in typical motherly fashion and say, You two.

Except, of course, that other times she seemed down on sex altogether. Like one time at supper she started going on about Mr. Beamish, a former real estate agent who started teaching English late in life, who everyone knows is gay. She said it was sick the way he was always roughhousing with Sid Moore, this very good-looking kid who may or may not be, though probably is, judging from the way he waltzes when he walks.

Barry, who is the most honest person I've ever met, started defending him. I used to wish I could be as honest as he is, but some of the things he says I could never say in a million years. Like he said he felt sorry for old Beamish, that it wasn't his fault that Nature had given him unconventional propensities, etc., etc. He said he could sympathize with anyone whose love was unrequited, which it would have to be in Mr. Beamish's case since he's about forty-five and looks exactly like Toad in *The Wind in the Willows*.

Then he looked at me and asked what *I* thought, but before I could say anything, Mom said, Oh, I have nothing against fantasizing, as long as it stops there. No doubt you find some of your students attractive, but you wouldn't go around wrestling with them on the quad. At least I hope you wouldn't. Barry said, Are you sure you're not getting all steamed up just because Beamish is a fag?

And then, right in the middle of putting a piece of potato in his mouth, he said he wouldn't mind roughhousing with Sid Moore himself, since he was the best-looking student on campus, male or female. At the time I went, Ooh, sick! and Mom said, Jesus, Barry, I wish you'd think before you said things like that, but Barry just blinked at us and went on eating. I'm just trying to be honest, he said. We all have homoerotic tendencies. Haven't you ever fantasized about making love with another woman?

Then they had one of their fights, so I went into the living room to read a book, and I heard Barry say, I never said I'd do anything—partly because I can't imagine Sid wanting to, and it's not in my nature to force someone to do something he or she doesn't want to. But you have to admit he's beautiful. If I let myself think about it, yeah, it turns me on. I'm not supposed to be turned on by Michelangelo's *David* just because I'm male? I don't see why it's so bad for her (meaning me) to hear. She's not a child. Mom said, It doesn't help at a very confusing time in her life to have you start equating love with sex, to which Barry replied, Who said anything about love, for Christ's sake?

I can remember a time—not so long ago—when Mom would have laughed it off or said something equally outrageous herself, but around the time I started going to R-rated movies and asking questions about them, she all of a sudden became very conservative about anything having to do with sex—except, of course, for women's rights and abortion.

Barry, on the other hand, is as much a radical as ever. He says in this day and age a teacher who wants to make his students think for themselves, and not just accept everything their teachers say, has to be subversive, which I tend to agree with.

His students all worship him even though he's one of the hardest graders in the school. They call him Comrade Lenin because he's always puffing on his pipe and saying stuff like, You don't really believe this bourgeois tripe? I've seen kids come out of his study crying because of what he wrote on their papers. On my friend Rachel's paper on *A Separate Peace* that she'd worked on for three days, he wrote, "This is bullshit. If *you* don't think, someone else is going to do your thinking for you." At first she hated him, but then she decided he was right.

But he's the most lenient member of the Disciplinary Committee, especially when it comes to victimless offenses like parietals and drugs. He and I smoked a joint once when Mom was in Washington, but that's another story. There were a whole bunch of us—we were on a canoe trip.

He doesn't have to teach, by the way. He's got tons of money from his mother and his aunts. But he wants to influence the younger generation to think for itself.

I think of Barry and my real father as kind of the same in some ways, even though I don't think they would have had that much in common. Barry would have thought of my dad as a "townie" because he grew up here in Wahaneeka and worked on the Trowbridges' farm. And my dad, I'm sorry to say, thinks that any *man* with long hair has to be a fag. But to me they both just seem young and vulnerable.

Except for Columbia University and the Peace Corps, Barry has spent his whole life at Steerforth Academy. It's his home, it's the father he never had—which is probably why he's never stopped being young himself and can relate so well to our generation.

We were reading Keats's "Ode on a Grecian Urn" in Ms. Plover's English class, and I couldn't help thinking of my two dads. "Forever panting, and forever young." That's my favorite poem. I was the only one in English 10 Honors who liked it, by the way. Everybody else probably thought I was brown-nosing, but I read Keats's letters, even though we didn't have to, and dreamt that I was Fanny Brawne and gave him a bottle of penicillin and he got better and sent me a postcard with a poem on it.

&
&&&

Mom was supposed to be in Boston for the day, shooting videos of the Pro-Abortion rally. She does free-lance documentaries, mostly about politics. Barry came back from his morning classes around noon. On Wednesdays school lets out in the middle of the day for sports, but I didn't go to sports that day. I was studying for a biology midterm that I already knew I was going to flunk.

What are you doing inside on such a lovely day? he said. It was Wednesday, February 29. I remember the sun was shining, the snow was melting, the whole world smelled fresh and clean. He said, You spend far too much time alone, E. Why don't you call up one of your friends? I held up my biology book. He threw a sneaker at me. Of making many books there is no end, he said. Much studying is a weariness of the flesh. It's one of his favorite sayings. A few minutes later he came back in and said, It's your mom's birthday Sunday. I haven't gotten her anything yet, have you? Want to go in on something together?

I think now that he was trying to be good. Trying to get us out of the house. Which made my heart go out to him all the more.

We can have lunch at the town diner, he called out, galumphing up the stairs to take his shower.

I remember I had a grilled-cheese sandwich for lunch, and afterwards he bought my mom a rainbow scarf and some very expensive earrings, which I picked out. He kept making me try on things, too, joking with the saleslady. Finally I bought some sunglasses, which I needed because my old ones were broken and the snow was so bright and pretty soon it would be spring. I wore them out of the store and felt like I was on a date with an older man. For the first time the word *affair* seemed to apply. We took the long way home, down by the river.

The house was empty. I went upstairs and lay down on my bed, which I often do when I'm supposed to be studying for a test. I closed my eyes.

After a while I heard water running in the upstairs bathroom. He was brushing his teeth. Then he rattled his knuckles on the doorjamb, the bed bounced, I opened my eyes, and he was sitting there *without any clothes on*! So, like a complete idiot, I shut my eyes again—like, I'm going to deal with this later—and rolled over on my stomach. My heart was going *boom, boom, boom.* I mean, I'd seen him without his clothes on before, since no one in my family is what you'd call modest, but this was a complete shock.

I kept thinking, What am I supposed to do now?

I pretended—if you can believe this—that I really was taking a nap. For a long time—about three or four minutes—we both just lay there on top of the covers, me completely dressed, my arms at my sides, trying to fake steady breathing, him naked as a walrus, which he looked like, sort of. Time had stopped. You could hear the snow dripping off the eaves, cars driving by.

After a while he said, You're not asleep.

Yes, I am, I said.

I could feel the bed moving. He lifted the hair away from my neck and started blowing warm air on my whatchamacallit—my nuque. Very gently. He touched me there with his lips—it wasn't quite a kiss.

I turned all the way over and looked at him. At his face, I mean.

What? he said softly.

I didn't know what, so I just looked at his eyes. He put his hand first on my stomach, then on my crotch. I froze. I was paralyzed. My heart was pounding in my ears.

He cleared his throat. This feel good? he asked stupidly.

Yes, I said, but don't. I don't know why I said don't. All of a sudden I felt mad at him for—well, because I didn't want him to act like I was a stupid little twit who had to be seduced or something. Led up to it. I wanted to be treated like a grown woman.

I gave him a mild version of my blue look, but I doubt if he noticed.

For about a thousand years we stayed like that. Then he started unbuttoning my shirt. I just lay there, not reacting. Not helping, but not hindering, either. To tell you the truth, I've never felt much one way or the other about my breasts. At first when he started touching them, it tickled. Then it just felt strange.

He started whispering in my ear, saying that *breast* was one of the nicest words in the English language, I can't remember why. Maybe because it rhymed with *nest*? I'd never given it any thought before. Then his hand starting making little excursions over my tummy. He goes, I just want to know what you call *that*, and put his hand between my legs again.

I kept looking at his face. It was semidark. He had shadows under his eyes.

He started whispering all the words for a woman's crotch, saying which ones he liked and why, none of which I'd ever thought about before. And then he took my hand, and I knew perfectly well what he was going to do with it. My heart was ringing like an alarm clock. In a dry sort of voice, he said, What's that? and I said, That's your penis, Barry.

He threw back his head and laughed like he was high or something. Then he started kissing me on the mouth like he'd gone crazy. I lay there wondering if he could taste the grilled-cheese sandwich on my breath.

Then the bed bounced up, and out of the corner of my eye I could see him putting on protection, making an adorable face. And then, another bounce, and I was in his arms, wishing I had seen more dirty movies because it was a lot harder than I thought and I kept worrying about not knowing what to do.

For example, it was almost impossible for me to relax, but if you don't relax—I mean, the man's so big. I kept crossing my legs and shouting, Stop! Not stop, but go slow. Barry, that hurts! Wait a second, will you? Don't move! I'm trying to relax.

I did the breathing exercises we learned in modern dance. I thought up some story problems in math.

Like if a man was such and such an age, and a girl considerably younger, well, ten years from now, although the difference in their ages would still be the same, it wouldn't matter as much because women in their twenties are often attracted to men in their thirties and even forties, and everybody just accepts them as a couple.

The whole time he was incredibly patient. This went on for it seemed like hours, and then I looked up and he was grinning. What? I said, laughing—we both started laughing.

It seems incredible now, but I actually laughed the whole time practically. Tears were running down my cheeks, making the pillow damp. The whole thing seemed so—weird. That adult people actually go around doing this all the time. And then, just as I was starting to imagine some people I know, naked and in bed together, Barry let out this long sigh and sort of collapsed on me. I remember his face was buried in the pillow, over my shoulder, so I put my arms around him and squeezed him with all my might. I felt so—proud.

Then from the hallway Mom said, E.? Barry? Anybody home? And the next thing we knew she was opening the door.

I don't see how I could have told any of this to Father Jude. I wanted to, but I was afraid he'd be grossed out. I also didn't want to squeal on my former stepdad, who was in enough trouble already. Just because I was officially underage doesn't mean he *molested* me or anything. Everything that happened was as much my fault as his. More. I knew even before that first night that he was attracted to me, and the day it happened I was supposed to be at field hockey practice but stayed home on purpose. I knew what I was doing.

I may be crazy, but I'm not stupid.

Mom's reaction was really scary. She went ape-shit, of course, but not right away. Not until her headshrinker told her it was all right for her to quote unquote own her anger. At first, like when she came into the room, and Barry and I were one flesh—one sweaty flesh—she didn't say or do anything. Barry lifted his head. Everybody looked at everybody else.

It was funny almost. I'm there going, Oh God, oh God, oh God.

I buried my head in the pillow for a count of ten, and when I looked again, she was gone.

We immediately jumped out of bed and started putting on our clothes as fast as we could. Or at least I did. For some reason Barry insisted on taking a shower. I remember thinking, This is getting crazier by the minute.

I mean how would that help, if we scrubbed our hard-to-get-at places and made them squeaky clean? We couldn't wash what we had done away, put on fresh underwear and pretend like everything was just the same.

I also couldn't not go looking for her. Not that I had an idea in the world what I was going to say. What can you say? I'm sorry, Mom. It won't happen again, I promise.

From behind the shower curtain Barry was telling me I should say we were *bundling* and that it wasn't as bad as it looked.

Right, Barry.

The front door was wide open; her car was still in the drive.

I started jogging around to all the places where I thought she might have gone, tucking my shirt in as I went. After about ten minutes I found her walking along the river. It's where she and I always used to go when we were depressed.

I wanted her to scream and holler, hit me or spit on me. Instead I had to fall in beside her, acutely aware of being taller than her.

I can't even begin to describe how I felt. I used to be a planet orbiting around the sun; now I was a comet heading for the earth.

I kept looking over at her, wondering what could possibly happen next. She looked old. I made the mistake of saying, How do you feel? and she said, Like nothing. Or maybe, Like a nothing.

And then she started ragging on herself, saying that she was a fool, a *fool*, a *goddamn fool*, that everybody else had probably known all along, probably pitied her, that first there was Sid Moore (I always wondered about that) and now her own daughter.

&
& &
&&&

Later on there was screaming and hollering—boy, was there ever. Just getting a divorce wasn't enough. She wanted Barry put away for life on charges of statutory rape. When her lawyer friend talked her out of that, saying it would be devastating for me, she went to see Mr. Smaller, the headmaster. She wanted them to fire Barry for—are you ready for this?—sexually harassing me.

About a year ago Steerforth adopted a policy against sexual harassment, which I guess is a good idea, even though almost immediately graffiti started appearing on the walls of the women's john to the effect of, I wish Mr. Fosdick would sexually harass me. (Actually my friend Jenny wrote some of it.)

But I really couldn't see how it was relevant in this case. I mean, Barry was not my official teacher. Even if I had asked for him, the school strongly discourages faculty children from taking their parents' classes.

Anyway, Mr. Smaller cried crocodile tears, said he felt awful for everyone concerned, especially me. But Barry, he said, was like a son to him. Something like this could ruin his career. And Barry, he reminded my mom, was widely recognized as one of the most innovative teachers in the history of Steerforth. He had taught a whole generation of young people how to think. I can't just fire him, he said. Not without a lot of awkward publicity. Think of the trauma to her (meaning me).

Let's be Christian, he suggested, and give him a second chance. I agree what he did was wrong.

But—but—Mom said. What about us?

I can just see Mr. Smaller spreading his hands apart. What was he going to say? I happened to be outside and could hear most of what Mom was screaming and yelling. So you're saying the victim is the one who should be punished? she shouted. Where are *we* supposed to go? How are *we* supposed to live? She started her I'm-a-single-parent-I've-had-to-raise-my-daughter-all-by-myself routine.

It was pretty embarrassing. People were walking by, saying, Hiya, E.! I'm there, trying to smile as pleasantly as I can. Oh, hi. Just my mom—shrug, smile. Trying to punish everyone, including herself. (In the old days she would have made me wear a big letter *A*. And she would have worn an *S*, for Sucker.)

Since no one in a position of authority seemed all that interested in punishing him, Mom threatened to take the law into her own hands. I don't know how serious she was, but more than once she talked about going over there (we were staying with the Lindbergs at the time) and cutting a certain part of his body off. I had to listen to this crap, since she was mainly trying to hurt me. She planned to use the Swiss Army knife I'd given her for Mother's Day.

Her face looked puffy. Strands of her hair were in her face.

At first I was really worried—for her, for myself. You don't know what she's like when she gets mad. Sometimes she starts shaking. And what about when that hatred got turned on me? What would she want to cut off of mine?

Sooner or later I did what every daughter has to do. From the kitchen drawer downstairs I got a butter knife. I stood at the bottom of the stairs and screamed with all my might that I was going to cut off one of my toes.

I started taking my shoes and socks off.

I remember as a kid being extremely fascinated by my mom's temper—at a certain age, more fascinated than afraid. I knew I wanted one, too, and found—at first much to my surprise—that I had it in me.

I can give people the evil eye, too. Pound my fists on the wall. Break things.

Mom came down the stairs in her nightie, crying and moaning. With her arms outstretched. Halfway down she said I was her precious. But the next morning she must have woken up with a hangover from all that shouting and weeping, because at breakfast she calmly announced that she'd arranged for me to have a talk with my old friend Peter Smilax of Boston, Massachusetts, who I hadn't seen in years.

Just a chat, she said, pouring herself a big mug of black coffee. If nothing came of it, I wouldn't ever have to go back, but it might be a relief to get some of the unexpressed hostility out of my system.

It was her way of punishing me for not wanting to cut my stepfather's patoogie off.

I honestly think sometimes that if she could have, my mom would probably have arranged for me to have my frontal lobes just slightly trimmed. After which maybe I would at last become the ideal daughter she's always longed for.

Well, I can tell you one thing: I'd rather have a bottle in front of me than a frontal lobotomy. (Ha ha. That's one of my Uncle Jimmy's jokes. I'm sorry if it's in poor taste.)

Because of everything I had done, I felt like I *had* to see Dr. Smilax, and, for a second or two, on the way to Boston, I even thought he might be able to say something that would help. But I just don't trust him. Even though from the way he swivels his chair and holds his clipboard loosely and looks out the window, he seems to be saying I'm above that filth, I can't help feeling that secretly he's obsessed with sex. Like, practically the first question he asked me—after we'd both gone through the nice-to-see-you-again routine and he, of course, went, My, my, you've grown up so much I hardly recognize you; you are becoming quite a young lady—was, What do you like to fantasize about when you are quote unquote sexually gratifying yourself?

Forgive me for saying so, but barf. Needless to say, I answered all his questions in monosyllables, like it was some kind of game. Yep. Nope. D'know.

I don't even want to think about any of that now. I came home feeling like a giant in a doll's house: I was so afraid that no matter what I did I was going to end up hurting someone.

Poor Mom's feelings for me were also complicated, I could tell. I couldn't ever just be her precious anymore.

Sometimes I felt like she was jealous of me.

Which is why sooner or later I had to get out of there, but that's another story.

Anyway, what I started to say is that Barry Comstock may not be a Boy Scout, but it isn't fair that he should be blamed for everything. Even Mom admits it's not his fault he's the way he is. She says that, in a way, he was abused as a child, growing up in a dysfunctional family where no one was ever honest about their emotions.

Barry Comstock, Sr., an orthodontist, ran off with his dental hygienist, leaving Mrs. C., a large, kind of out-of-it woman, to get what affection she could from her little boy. So of course he grew up thinking he was the prince of all that he surveyed.

Someone like that appeals to the mother in all of us, Mom said. I don't really hate him. Naturally I'm mad at him. Mostly I just feel sorry for him. He needs help.

He needs help—my mom's absolute worst curse.

You're lonely, she said. In too big a hurry to grow up.

Between clenched teeth, I said, Don't Analyze Me.

Mom may not have hated him, but she literally refused to talk to him, unless her boyfriend-lawyer was there as a witness. And if I said the least thing in Barry's favor—like that I didn't see why I couldn't just go over and ask him for my Walkman back, since the two of them had given it to me for my birthday and he certainly wasn't going to try to keep it just to get even with us—she immediately started talking in the sort of hushed voice you use with retarded people, saying I shouldn't blame myself for anything that might have happened, since that was a classic symptom of abused children.

It was all right to hate the son of a bitch, she said.

At the hearing Barry's attorney tried to prove that she wasn't exactly an angel, either, that she and her lawyer friend were in Boston together the same day Barry and I were making love.

Mom vehemently denies they were doing anything wrong, says lawyers always try to dredge up dirt.

I wouldn't hold it against her if it was true, except that I really think she's making a mistake in the object of her affections. I wish she'd find someone who is worthy of her, for a change, instead of a model from an Eddie Bauer catalog. She deserves a good man, someone like her first husband.

I asked her once, naively, about child custody. That was a thermonuclear reaction I should have seen coming. With that Humbert Humbert? Etc., etc.

She didn't understand my question. All I meant was, Did *I* have to move in with Les Smith, since I was never going to be able to think of him as my dad? Couldn't I just stay at Steerforth as a boarder and come home on holidays?

Barry started acting really paranoid around me, like he thought I wanted to harm him.

I went up to him during the divorce proceedings. What

do you want from me? he said. In this really strained voice. Nothing, I said, backing away. He didn't look the same. He looked like other men his age.

Would you still be able to root for me, Father Jude, if you knew all this? And not just because it's your job and you have to?

My real dad knows, by the way. I didn't give him a blow-by-blow description, just the main points. At first he looked sad, like he wished he'd never gone off to the war and gotten killed. Then he put his skinny arm around me and whispered, "You can stay with me, Effie."

There's m
ore: an
other c
onfessi
on&&&&&

&

Hey, Jude, don't let me down,
you have found her, now go and get her.
Remember to let her into your heart,
then you can start
to make it better. . . .

Sorry about that! I pretend I'm writing this to you, even
though I'm not, because it feels kind of crazy if you just
write to yourself. By the way, you don't look like a
priest—has anyone ever told you that? I mean it as a com-
pliment. Not that I know what a priest should look like,
but he shouldn't have such bushy eyebrows and such a
boisterous laugh. Maybe you should have been a bartender
or something, ha ha.

I don't know if I've ever told you this before, but when I
first read Shakespeare's *Hamlet* I thought *I* was Hamlet.

Don't laugh; when you first read the Bible, you probably thought you were Jesus Christ. I went around in black tights giving soliloquies all the time, mostly about people who "post with such dexterity to incestuous sheets," and other equally obnoxious and snotty things—I think my mom was on her third marriage at the time. She told me to cut it out, already, so then I sent away to some Shakespeare festival in Canada for a poster of the Prince of Denmark and hung him up on my bedroom wall. Nice buns.

I've read *Hamlet*, I think five times, and even though I know the supposed outcome, each time I hope and pray that he'll make the right decision, for a change, and that it will all end happily. He'll marry Ophelia, who won't drown herself, and so on and so forth.

Jerks in my class said she was the Renaissance stereotype of a dumb woman, but look at what she says to her brother when he's about to leave for France. She's not dumb—in love, maybe. And Hamlet isn't crazy. He's this very sensitive guy—that's the tragedy. If he were alive today, he would probably be a rock musician, and then people wouldn't be in such a hurry to condemn him. And I, in spite of my strict feminist upbringing, would be his number one groupie.

&&

Last night I dreamt that everyone was chasing me—my mom, the lady from Planned Parenthood, Barry Comstock. We were in a field, and I know this is sick, but Barry didn't have any clothes on. I tried not to look, but when a man is running around not wearing anything, you can't exactly not notice.

Also, the doctor in his long white coat—he was there. I didn't see him at first because he was lying in the grass. But then he sat up, and at first I thought he had bagpipes on one shoulder. He got up and started chasing me, too, only all the hoses and attachments kept sliding down his arm and, luckily for me, he had to keep stopping to adjust them.

I just realized who he was: Michael Palin, the one on "Monty Python" who always has a crazed smile, even when something awful is happening.

I ran as fast as I could, knowing that there was a cliff somewhere and that if I slipped and fell over the edge, I would fall about a hundred miles into Lake Michigan glimmering below.

You and my dad were the only ones on my side. Over here, E., you called. Quick, over here!

I tried to get to you, zigzagging back and forth, but at the last minute I made the mistake of looking around to see where the edge of the cliff was and ran straight into my mother's arms. She hugged me tight while Barry tied my hands behind my back with a pair of her old panty hose. Then they dragged me over to this pile of rocks and held me down.

It was very beautiful there, in an austere sort of way. There were chunks of granite sticking up out of the ground, all covered with yellow lichen. Tufts of spiky grass were growing all around.

Since there was nothing I could do, I just lay there and watched. It was almost a relief, having it over with. The doctor went on smiling his crazy smile, even though he was having a terrible time disentangling his machine—I realize now it looked like our old vacuum cleaner. Mom had to untangle it for him. She was pissed, I could tell. Barry unwound the cord and went behind some rocks to plug it in. It began to hum.

One of the hoses was bigger than the others, and corrugated. They opened the end up and tried pushing my head inside, but it wouldn't fit. Then Mom, shaking with impatience, put her hand over my nose and mouth. . . .

Today is Sunday, September 9. I hereby swear, before God and man, that by sundown tonight I shall go to the nearest crossroads and kiss the ground (that's the easy part). Then I have to confess my sins, like the murderer in *Crime and*

Punishment. It has to be *in public* or at least out loud to somebody *real.* And it has to be the whole truth, not just what I've written down so far.

No chickening out, or else!

No sooner had I written the above than I heard church bells ringing, so I quickly chewed one of my shoelaces in half and used the longer piece to fasten the front of my jeans, which have grown too tight to snap. Then I hurried to this church called Zion's Home. People all dressed up in suits and fancy dresses kept arriving in cars, which they parked along the highway.

At the door two women were shaking everybody's hand, acting friendly in that impersonal way Christians have, which was fine with me. They asked me whose daughter I was, and I said Jephthah's. One of them said her name was Ruth Sawyer, and the other one I think was Grace. They introduced me to some people who were just arriving, whose names I don't remember, and everybody shook hands.

Unfortunately it was some kind of Protestant church—I still haven't figured out how you tell the difference. Grace said, What did you say your name was? I said, Elizabeth, but my voice, which is getting rusty from disuse, sounded squeakier than ever.

I kept waiting for the right moment to confess, but first we sang a lot of hymns, and then the preacher, who looked like this grizzly bear I saw chained up in a garbage dump once, rushed up onto the stage and started reading the part in the Bible about how there's a time for this and a time for that. I've always loved that part, but to tell you the truth, I've never understood it.

I mean, I understand about the seasons, and how there's a time and a place for everything, and the sun also rises, etc. But is all that supposed to be happy or sad? And what if you're one of the ones who was making love when you were supposed to be making war or vice versa? God wouldn't take it out on your children, would he?

Whenever anybody's up there blathering away and I'm supposed to be listening, all sorts of questions start occurring to me and I lose my concentration, so it's a good thing I'm not in school. It's like I can only absorb one thing, but that's enough to start my mind thinking down a certain channel, and then I have no idea what else they've been talking about.

For example, the preacher started discussing opposites, and okay, adjectives are fairly obvious, but like what's the opposite of a noun, like *mother* or *daughter*? And can a word be the opposite of itself—like *love* for instance? What does opposite mean exactly?

The opposite of *baby* is *ash*.

I had to bite my lip to keep from laughing because my dad was sitting there, doing a crossword puzzle on the bulletin. One of the clues was "opposite of war," five letters, and he wrote *house*. But what made me laugh was, when he put on his glasses to see the fine print, he looked exactly like Mr. Potato Head. That's when it dawned on me that the preacher was looking right at me, asking me something.

I stood up. It was now or never. I took a deep breath and said, I'm an awful person, but I said it in such a low voice that I don't think anyone heard.

Still, the whole audience started muttering and groaning.

150

The preacher motioned for me to come up, so I started squeezing down my row. When I got to the aisle, I bowed three times, like Raskolnikov. But then like a moron I lost my nerve and made a run for it. I pushed open the heavy wooden door. Outside was just country, and I hurried along for at least a mile, every once in a while looking over my shoulder to see if anyone was chasing me.

I can't say I feel that much better for having gone to church. I must not be a religious person or whatever. I liked the hymns, though, and kept humming them to myself as I picked some toadstools to eat in case I don't *really* confess by sundown—just kidding, ha ha.

&
&&&

My dad (or what's left of him) and I went and stood on the kitchen porch of the house next door and knocked as quietly as we could—and still call it a knock, I mean. I was kind of hoping the people that used to live here had moved away, so I could say, At least I tried. But their name was on the mailbox in big drippy letters: TROWBRIDGE. I cleared my throat a hundred times and spit about a million.

These would be the first living people I had talked to in several days.

I must have stood there, rocking on the big slab stoop

that's coming loose from the house, for a full five minutes, my knocks getting louder and louder, now that I was pretty sure no one was home, when without warning a chicken darted out of the bushes and pecked me on the toes of my sneakers.

Do they always do that, or was it some kind of cosmic sign?

Then I looked up, and there was Mrs. Trowbridge's old face frowning at me through the kitchen door. She looked exactly like the photograph of Bertrand Russell that Barry Comstock keeps in his classroom. I said I was Richard's daughter, but it didn't seem to register one way or the other. So I shouted, WE'RE JEHOVAH'S WITNESSES, and she let us in.

She must have an advanced case of Alzheimer's disease, because she was only wearing a slip and her hair had dust in it. Also, the television was on in the other room, and most of the time she seemed to be paying more attention to it, through the arched doorway, than she was to me. Especially whenever there was a commercial on.

I can't remember if I've told you about the Trowbridges. They were my dad's foster parents. His real parents abandoned him when he was a little kid, and he lived in an orphanage for a while. Not even my mom knows all the details, because she said he didn't like to talk about it. But eventually he came to stay on the Trowbridges' farm. And when he was of legal age, he dropped out of school and worked for Mr. T., in exchange for his room and board.

Which is how he and my mom met. She went next door to use their phone one day, he happened to be sitting at the table, and *boing!* I know the whole story, even the lovey-dovey parts, like how he came by with a bottle of wine that night and she let him kiss her on the lips.

But I don't want to bore you.

Mrs. T. mentioned, by way of greeting, that her husband had run off with a floozy a few years back. I don't know what come over him, she said, clucking like a chicken, but when I went down in the basement there was all these pictures of nekked women. Also quote unquote thinga-mabobs. She offered to take us on a tour, but we said that was okay.

According to her, the whole world has gone sex crazy, so, needless to say, we kept our mouths shut.

We sat down at this rickety kitchen table, and she gave me a glass of water in a plastic cup and a peach a little the worse for wear, which I devoured in one bite.

Maybe there's a spark of understanding in there? You never can tell with people when they get like that.

I told her I was on the verge of a breakdown, and she goes, That's nice, dear.

I shouted—because she's also a little deaf—MRS. T., I'M EXPECTING! and she starts beaming and nodding like that's the best news she's had in ages.

So then, sucking on the peach pit, I said, Mrs. T., I've come to confess.

I took a deep breath and told her that from the day my mom walked in on us, with our proverbial pants down, Barry and I hadn't had a single chance to be alone and talk. Because first Mom went ape-shit and instead of listening to Barry, who said, Look, I think we should all go for counseling, just went on throwing our books into the boxes she had gotten from the New Hampshire State Liquor Commission. Sitting on the floor with her hair undone. And then we had to move in with the Lindbergs, who are this really sweet old physics teacher emeritus and his wife who rattle around all day in a colonial house that's way too big for them, apparently unaware of the tragedy in their midst.

She made me promise never to go back to *his* house alone, so of course I promised.

But I figured that sooner or later he'd find a way to get in touch with me. I mean, it would be too unreal if one minute we were that intimate and the next—*nada*. I made at least a hundred trips to my mailbox in the student post office, and after a week of finding my box empty, I left a note in his.

Actually it was a poem called "Boris Pasternak Dies in His Sleep," because I was reading *Dr. Zhivago* at the time, in the hopes of getting my mind off my problems, only it had the opposite effect. And on the book jacket it said that the author had died in his sleep, so I couldn't help wondering what that would be like, sometimes half-wishing I could go that way.

I mean, would you be just having a dream or something, like about fishing over the side of a boat, when suddenly the looming shadow under the bow, the swelling wave, the tug on the line turned out to be Death? And it caught you, instead of the other way around.

It also said that Pasternak had a mistress, and his wife knew about her and everything. Those Russians are so sensible!

Anyway, the poem was a veiled reference to our situation, and I know that he has to have gotten it because when I went back after my fourth-period class that day, his box was empty. But he didn't reply. He didn't send it back with comments on it, like he usually did when I showed him something I had written.

Don't ask me what I was expecting. The nearest I came to actually planning anything was that we could sail around the world for a couple of years on a boat that he could easily afford to buy (Barry and me, not Boris). Living on seafood. And that he could teach me everything he knew—which is a lot—so my precious education wouldn't get stunted. And under his guidance I would blossom into a remarkable young poet. If you want to know the truth, I was planning to use the line about Pasternak as the title of my first book. Oh, I didn't have any illusions. It was going to be a very modest book. Mostly about death—ha ha. (You have to admit it's a good title, better than most of the crap you see.)

I tried to be realistic, being careful to also imagine the

hard work of sailing, since I've been the crew on a boat before and know the kind of stuff you have to do. In my imagination we were in a state of perpetual near-nakedness, running sails up the main mast, squatting to avoid getting beaned when the whatchamacallit came around, peeing in an empty soup can.

Our tanned skin seasoned with salt, Barry's legs, etc.

From distant and exotic ports we could send back postcards to our loved ones.

Mom was the one catch. Maybe in a year or two, after the shock of finding us was a thing of the past, she would come to accept us??? The way you do, even things that at first seem outrageous. I mean, that's the story of *my* life, learning to accept weird things, so why can't other people, for a change?

But for some reason I could never picture her welcoming us home with open arms.

You could say that Mom was the reality my fantasy always ran aground on. That and the fact I always get seasick.

I discovered something else: You can want two things at the same time. I mean, really want them badly. So much that it hurts. And I mean two things that you can't have both of, because they sort of cancel each other out.

I wanted (1) to make my mom feel okay again and not bring any more gray hairs down on her head and (2) to figure out a way for what had started between Barry and me to continue forever.

The answer I came up with was to be discreet about it, which is the moral lesson Steerforth Academy tries to inculcate in all its students. You know, you can smoke all the hash you want in the woods, as long as you don't get caught. Only nerds get caught (and therefore deserve to get kicked out).

Voilà. Nobody had said we couldn't go on at least being friends. Having our own necessarily secret relationship. The way any mature adults would.

Sex could be a separate issue, something to be worked out later. On our sailboat we could sleep in different berths?

I knew what I wanted to do, but not how to do it, which was why *we* had to talk. And since our minds ran parallel on almost everything, I couldn't help thinking he was probably arriving at the exact same conclusion. Looking for a way to get in touch with me, too.

I must have crisscrossed the quad a thousand times, in the hopes of running into him. I couldn't just go and knock on the side door of our old house, since I had promised my mom I wouldn't, but she hadn't said anything about us accidentally meeting on the campus walk.

I hung around for hours with *Dr. Zhivago* under my arm in all the places he and I used to go together, no doubt enhancing my reputation as a dweeb, but I didn't care.

Mrs. T. chuckled to herself. I glanced up, startled, to see if it was me or the television.

And then on the night of March 14, I went on, two weeks to the day after the first time we made love—sort of our anniversary—there was a light on in his classroom. Which meant he was up there, working on the Great American Novel.

Whereas just a couple of weeks ago it would have seemed like the most natural thing in the world, to be going up the stairs to see my stepfather and mentor, for some reason I felt like a criminal or something. The lights they always leave on in the hallway seemed to be ringing.

The door was ajar. I tapped three times with my pinky knuckle.

He looked up when I walked in like he was half-expecting me, so I felt this surge of well-being. He put his pen down, got up, and walked over to where I was standing. Not saying a word the whole time. He turned the light out and helped me take my coat off. Then he reached for my hand, like he wanted to shake it, and led me over to his desk, which is in this little alcove off to one side.

For a long time—three minutes?—we just stood there, looking at each other's faces. Like we were trying to read each other's thoughts. Finally I got up on my tippy toes and kissed him. At first he just stood there, immobile, but on the third try he kissed me back. Then it felt so familiar, so all right again.

(Mom was miles away, centuries away, mythological.)

In the semidark I couldn't tell what his expression was, or what, if anything, he was trying to say. He wasn't happy and he wasn't sad. Appraising, I guess.

I had to be the one to make all the first moves, initiate everything. So I started whispering stuff like, I've missed you so much, darling, we have to plan, okay? I told him we had to find a way to put our love into practice, but without hurting anyone else. I gave him an abbreviated version of how maybe we could go on a long trip together.

Then, because he was just standing there like a statue, I put his arms around me and got him to hold me. And immediately when I felt his rough whiskers on my face, I felt so safe, like no matter what happened at least he and I would always be together. And we would be everything to

158

each other, like he said—friends, teachers, fathers and mothers—even lovers, if fate willed it.

Sort of rubbing my whole body against his, like we were slow dancing, I said, Say something. So in a sort of rusty voice—not a whisper—he said, Does your mom know you're here? and, When was your last period?

I want to be absolutely honest, so nobody gets a mistaken impression about anything. I didn't mind it one bit when he turned me around, like we were still dancing, and started hugging me from behind with all his might. His curly head against my back. His teeth gentle on my shoulder. He caressed me like he never had before.

I was on one of the moons of Jupiter.

And when I realized he wanted to make love again—which didn't come as a complete surprise—I didn't *say*, Barry, do you think it's a good idea? Or, What if she's been following me and at the last minute climbs in the window? Or, Shouldn't you be wearing some kind of protection?

I know, I know, not smart. All my life I've read "Ann Landers" and "Ask Beth" and thought, What a lot of dumb girls there are in the world, but at the time I thought, It's March so the odds are 31 to 1 against. If something happened, I figured I'd adjust. It would be the beginning of something new. Of our adventure together.

Yeah, we made love again, only this time it was different. I'm sitting here, wondering how to describe it. It was like the Whoosh, a carnival ride I went on a couple of weeks ago, when I was feeling reckless and didn't give a damn what happened and was half-hoping some boy would pick me up. And at first, while people were getting on, I was high on the sheer daringness of it, sitting alone in my little swinging car, screaming in anticipation. But then the machine started, swinging up higher than I wanted it to and dropping out from under me so suddenly that I thought I was going to get killed. And there'd been a sign warning pregnant women not to ride.

At first, standing there in his classroom, with a little wind rattling the windowpanes, it was everything I ever wanted, feeling him lean against me. But then for some reason I couldn't get comfortable. Maybe I just wasn't in the mood, or maybe I'm not good at it, but it was like we were drifting more apart than ever. Which made me feel like I was a—don't laugh—utensil or something.

I said, Barry, you're kind of hurting me.

I said, Couldn't we lie on the floor?

I would have been more turned on if we had just kissed and fooled around. Or if he hadn't been so angry or passionate or whatever. But at least I was giving him pleasure. I was glad of that.

Except that I'm not sure he was having that great a time, either, since he kept huffing and puffing, shuffling into different positions, sort of pinching my breasts.

Finally he said in my ear, Say the F-word.

That struck me as a good idea, as weird as everything else that was happening in that dark classroom. Think about it: if his students could have seen us! So I started saying the F-word, over and over, louder and louder. Like the Little Engine That Could. And it seemed to help because after a few minutes he let out this blast of air and nearly crushed me against the desk.

After a few seconds I wriggled around in his arms. I reached up and put my hand on his cheek. Hold me, I said. But he was already handing me his handkerchief, hurriedly putting himself back together like it had only now dawned on him that Mr. Gresham, the janitor, might still be in the building, going from room to room, switching on the lights. Not that there was any sound of anybody banging metal baskets out in the hall.

I didn't see why he should care now. Kiss me thirty-four times, I said.

He brushed his mouth against my cheek.

I didn't know how to read him. Are you all right? I asked, because while he was catching his breath, he held his hand on his chest like he was having a heart attack or something, his eyes glittering.

That's got to be the dumbest thing any two people have ever done, he said, looking at me strangely.

I felt my teeth glowing in the dark. I know, I said, cheerfully.

But he meant it in a bad way.

You shouldn't have come up here, he said. Don't anymore.

I started to explain that I hadn't meant for that to happen, either, but didn't express myself very well. But at least he interrupted me in a nicer voice.

Me, neither, he said. It was nobody's fault. Only you'd better go, before your mother shows up with her video camera. And, please, E., don't come back.

Barry, I said, hugging him. I'm willing to do anything, go anywhere, just as long as we can be friends. This is bigger than both of us, a marriage of true minds, etc.

Quit it, he said, laughing unhappily. Don't drag poor Will into it.

He stroked the hair out of my eyes and touched my nose, I think fondly.

You really do mean a lot to me, he said. More than you'll ever know. But this is wrong and—spitting sound— stupid. In a couple of years, you'll find someone more your age. And then maybe some of your sweet dreams really will come true. I already envy you both.

I still hadn't explained *anything*, but he held my lips together.

No speeches. Just go. For everybody's sake.

It was like I was his goddamn student or something, and now he was dismissing me. Or like he was following some recipe he had gotten out of the *Reader's Digest* for "How To Be a Good Stepfather."

Have a good life, he called out after me, but when I turned around to see if he was kidding, he snarled, Scram!

So I scrammed. I scrammed all the way home, wishing real tears would fall, wishing when I got home I could throw open the door, sobbing, and have Mom say, My poor sweet baby, what is it? and leave her work to sit with me on the couch and stroke my hair while I told her all the crap I'd been going through.

Ha! Instead, I was weirdly self-possessed and sober. Not self-possessed, because I didn't feel like myself. I couldn't find myself in this experience.

I was a girl without a country.

And then, because in fact the Lindbergs live only a couple of blocks away, I really was closing the front door behind me, my alien head full of cunning and lies.

That's when I first became the liar I am to this day, I said, and Mrs. T. went, Whew, and fanned herself with her hand.

Mom was in the Lindbergs' den, in front of this fancy

monitor she has for mixing and matching videos. She had probably been watching everything on her magic screen like the Wicked Witch of the West in *The Wizard of Oz*, but if so, she didn't let on. A part of me felt like we were enemies now, and would be for the rest of our lives.

I'm all sweaty, I called from the stairs.

She just looked at me absentmindedly and smiled.

I took off my clothes piece by piece, sniffing every thread before burying them deep inside the hamper. My undies I washed out with soap and hot water and hung over the radiator. In the shower I made beards of lather between my legs. Somewhere deep inside I hurt. As if one of those organs you just have to accept on faith that you have, like my liver, had been bruised.

Well, you know the rest. That was the fourteenth of March, six months minus five days ago. When my period didn't come and didn't come, I went and stood on Gallants' hill—it was during a thunderstorm—and vowed, whatever else happened, I would *never* get an abortion.

Mrs. Trowbridge laughed and laughed, bowing her head to the table.

I had to laugh, too, I'm not sure why.

I didn't seem to be able to explain any of this to anybody else, I said, but maybe you can understand?

She made a looping motion with her head, sort of like she was nodding, but her gaze had wandered back through the archway into the other room where on the screen a woman, immaculately dressed and wearing too much makeup, was screaming at a man too good-looking to be real. There was organ music in the background.

I knew Mrs. T. could only have about as much presence of mind as the half-empty Coke bottle on her kitchen table, which is the audience they aim for on television, but I didn't care. It was such a relief to be finally telling someone the truth, the whole truth, and nothing but the truth, so help me God.

I said, I have to go to the bathroom. Will you excuse me? Is this the way?

Fortunately or unfortunately there was a commercial on, so she only smiled blankly.

I hurried upstairs, being careful to climb over the little piles of junk that adorned every step. And I really did use the bathroom, being careful to make as many running-water noises as I could. Then I quickly snuck down the hall, opening all the doors, until in the back of the house I found a room with a single bed and some dusty rocks on the floor alongside the wall and a hornets' nest hanging from a branch someone had nailed to the ceiling.

I can't say conclusively that it was my father's room, all covered with dust and smelling like old shoes, since the Trowbridges took in a series of foster boys. But I assumed it was. And I can't begin to tell you what it felt like to be standing in the room where my dad used to walk around, put his pajamas on, think his living thoughts when he was my age.

Yes, I can: It felt the same way it did the one time in my life I shoplifted, which much to my surprise turned me on in a—ahem—sick way. I'm sorry, but that's the honest-to-God truth. It must be some kind of biological short circuit between the sex part of the brain and the stealing part. Which I'm sure is why so many lonely girls shoplift.

If I ever go back to Virginia, I plan to make restitution. It was a maternity bra, and I was too embarrassed to march up to the cashier and have her ring it up. Boy, you start confessing one sin, and the next thing you know all your sins come dancing out like a chorus line of paper dolls.

I guess that has to be pretty evil, huh? To feel that way when you're standing in your own father's room. All I can say in my own defense is that since I never knew my dad, it was more like being in the room of a boy I had secretly liked all my life. Opening the closet, I put my hot face in among the shirts and breathed in the atticky smell and felt like I wanted to steal everything.

But how could I hide it all under my shirt?

I peeked in all the shoe boxes, drawers, under the bed. Sick, I know. It embarrasses me to write this down, even if nobody ever reads it. I even started taking the few books there were out of the shelves and riffling the pages, in the hopes he had signed his name or put little stars in the margin like I do when I read something I really like. But unfortunately they were all Hardy Boys books and *Popular Mechanics* and something called *Engineering Dreams*.

Then I looked up, and naturally Mrs. T. was standing in the doorway. I couldn't tell whether she was mad or not—she was sort of shaking all over. So I went and got her tepid hand and made her sit down on the bed. And then I plopped down beside her and began talking in a loud, clear voice, the way you do to a scared child, being very careful to explain everything so that she would understand.

I began by saying that she was my spiritual grandmother, which in a way she is, since she helped raise my dad. I smoothed her hair and told her I had always believed he was still alive—that at least his soul was—and that I used to imagine him up in the box of this fancy theater, peering over the velvet railing. Whenever I got an *A* on a paper or was nice to a retard, he would start whistling and clapping his hands. But if I did something bad, he would lean back slightly so I couldn't see his face.

I told her what Dr. Smilax had said about him being my superego. Actually I can't remember exactly what he said, just that he sounded sad—like that the late Sigmund Freud would be disappointed if he knew.

But being told that didn't make him go away. Nothing did, until the second time with Barry. This is hard to explain, but after that, I could still see the ornate box, except that now it was empty. At first I assumed I had killed my father's immortal soul, but then I started seeing him everywhere, at the window of the den, out in the garage, in the live oak out back. I would run to the front door, and there he would be in his old car by the curb, his sad eyes peering out. So that must have meant he had come down from wherever to help me!

Then we got on the subject of babies, and I told her how my mom is fanatically Pro-Choice, but every time I announced my choice she tried to talk me out of it. And Barry sent me more than enough money to pay for an abortion. No note, just a check—so he could write it off as an expense on his income tax? Under what, child support???

By the way, this same individual had the nerve to say in a letter to S. Leicester (Les) Smith that he thought I was being vindictive, which I did not appreciate, to put it mildly. But then the lady at Planned Parenthood said practically the same thing, so maybe there was some truth in it, at first.

But Mom kept saying just the opposite, that I had a moral right to get an abortion because my stepfather had quote unquote molested me—as if getting an abortion was a legitimate way of getting even with him.

All summer she kept acting incredibly motherly towards me—to impress on me that I was still a child. In her eyes I had to be *the victim* and not *the other woman* who could maybe turn her husband on in ways she couldn't. That sounds really snotty, but how are you supposed to tell your own mother, especially when she keeps trying to help you find a convenient scapegoat, that you weren't molested, that the whole time you knew perfectly well what you were doing?

After a while I had to stop listening to her, if I really was going to be responsible. It was my choice only if I chose. So I said, Barry Comstock can go—*expletive deleted*—himself. This doesn't have anything to do with him anymore.

Mrs. T. put a wadded-up Kleenex to her mouth and coughed.

I studied her for signs of intelligence but couldn't be sure.

It was least of all the fetus's fault, but now I should take it out on her, let them do what they wanted to her so I

167

could go back to my normal, my promising life? To the decided unamusement of everyone but me, I started calling her Iphigenia, i.e., Effie. The fetus, I mean.

In case you don't know, Iphigenia's the one whose throat they slit so the winds would blow and they could sail their ships to Troy and nuke the fother-muckers back to the Stone Age—though according to this one book of myths I have by Robert Graves, she may have been rescued at the last minute by the ever-resourceful Artemis, who carried her off to safety in a far-off land. They left a little deer at the altar in her place.

Mom kept saying, What about college? All your friends are going to be going off to college next year, and you're going to be stuck at home, taking care of your baby. She said it with her lips out like it was something awful, *bay-bee.*

It was very noble, etc., to want to do the right thing, to make what the lady at Planned Parenthood called The Noble Gesture, but could I, at my young age, have any idea what it meant to be a mother?

So then Mom got this bright idea, I think from one of those psychobabble magazines she's always reading, of having me carry an egg around for twenty-four hours. So I could see what it felt like to have something fragile dependent on you all the time. Only it backfired because I got very attached to my egg and nearly had hysterics when she suggested we boil it.

I had to do what I had to do, whether it was convenient or reasonable or any of those good things, because whether I liked it or not, Effie was already in there. There was this little creature growing inside me, and maybe she wasn't an official person yet, and according to the laws of the land I could still get my womb vacuumed out and afterwards we could all go out for a sundae—which is what my friend in Virginia, Stacey Fine, did. And God wouldn't strike me dead—he didn't strike Stacey Fine, whose boyfriend got her pregnant, dead. She said it wasn't even that big a deal. I'm not saying I know what anybody else should do. I'm not a Pro-Lifer. It's just that there was no way *I* could do it. I mean, I read up on it, and at three months, which is only halfway through the time you can legally get an abortion, they can already hear noises and suck their transparent thumbs.

&
&&&
&&&

At the beginning of the summer we moved to Virginia, and then, practically before I knew it, it was getting to be late August, and school starts early in Fairfax County, the following Monday, in fact. School never worried me all that much because Mom bullied the principal into saying I could take a leave of absence and do my work at home.

But I was worried about my power to hold out against everybody else's opinion indefinitely. Deep down I was sure I was right, but it was kind of scary that *nobody* else agreed with me, except for the Catholic church and some crackpot fundamentalists who got my name from somewhere and came to pray with me. I mean, what if at the last minute—which is twenty-four weeks, or the end of your second trimester, when some babies can survive outside the womb—what if at the last minute they talked me into it?

And then Mom found a Dr. Ivan the Terrible (not his real name—I immediately blanked out his real name), who specialized in cases of psychological stress. She had tentatively made an appointment for me. But don't feel you have to see him, she said. You can call and cancel. His number is on the pad by the phone. It wouldn't hurt to have him evaluate your situation. Check on the fetus.

I took the money Barry sent me and dragged my guitar and my backpack into downtown Washington. My friend Stacey wanted me to buy her a pair of handcuffs, as a present for her boyfriend, who's always bugging her to try weird stuff. So I browsed around in Mike's Joke Shop on the corner of Fourteenth and M streets, but when I saw them hanging on a hook, even though I knew they just wanted them to fool around with, my heart misgave me, and I got her a whoopy cushion instead. (Her taste, not mine.)

I was thinking of getting myself a mask, now that I was becoming an outlaw, but all they had, besides the usual monsters and werewolves, were Richard Nixon and Ronald Reagan. The shop must be run by a bunch of Democrats.

I would have preferred JFK, since he's the one I identify with. He got killed when he was still young, too. Plus, he's the one who led us into Vietnam, or at least that's what our last-year history and politics teacher said. She took great delight in telling us he wasn't as great a president as everybody thinks, mainly because he was always sneaking around—oh, the horror! the horror!—having affairs with people like Marilyn Monroe and I can't remember who else.

I got the Nixon because it was reduced. Forty percent off.

Then, since I happened to be in the neighborhood, I went into the Greyhound Bus station, which has to be one of the scuzziest places in North America, and sat down on one of those wooden benches that have a puddle of you-hope-it's-Sprite on one side and a bum curled up on the other. Actually I felt perfectly safe in there, since everybody else was too stoned to care one way or the other.

I sat there and hugged my guitar case, like the immature child I was then, wishing someone would tell me what to do. So at first I wasn't paying that much attention to what the voice on the loudspeaker was saying, but then it started listing all the places where the next bus was going—BALT-imo'r, HARR-isbu'g, PITTS-bu'g, CAN-tun, AK-run, CLEVE-lund, TO-leedo, DE-troy't. . . .

Pricking up my ears, I thought, Detroit? That's where my dad's from. My mom, too. My grandma lives in the suburbs. Dot, dot, dot.

From Ohio I sent my mom a postcard, telling her not to worry, but it's harder than it sounds to run away from people who love you and vice versa.

After Detroit—promise not to ever tell my mom?—I hitchhiked. And despite what everyone tells you about what a cinch it is to get picked up, especially if you're a girl, most people just give you a dirty look and drive right

171

by. The first night I had to sleep out under the trees and nearly froze my patoogies off. And then this one guy who picked me up started saying he had had lots of girlfriends, but never one as young and cute as me. I told him I had AIDS and started snapping my teeth, and when we stopped at the next red light, I bolted from the car and took refuge in a fair. It started to rain and, well, you know the rest. Late that night President Nixon was found sleeping in the Twemlows' bed, I guess because he's too ashamed to sleep in his own, ha ha.

I wonder sometimes if the baby can still be alive in there, after everything that's happened, but then she gives me a good kick in the appendix so I won't lose heart.

Mrs. T. giggled. We stood up and went downstairs. I had one of my dad's shirts wadded up under my arm.

We're your new neighbors, I said in the kitchen, because I could tell she had no idea who we were. I thought this might cheer her up, and it seemed to.

I had to shout, WE JUST MOVED IN, NEXT DOOR. THAT'S MY DAD. HIS NAME IS HARVEY.

Ooh, she goes, clapping her hands.

Then she made what for her was a speech. Wouldn't you like some eggs? she said. They're fresh.

She gave them to us nested in paper toweling in a coffee can, and they really were fresh. I never used to like eggs, but when I got home they tasted so good I started blubbering.

When I moved to Virginia, I made friends with Stacey Fine, not because we're soul mates or anything like that, but because she's always in trouble with her parents, too. Her boyfriend rides a motorcycle and leaves his empty beer bottles in the street.

To tell you the truth, I think she has serious problems. She talks back to her mom but takes incredible abuse from Alex—that's his name.

But at least around her I didn't feel so much like—an extraterrestrial.

I remember one time we were sunbathing on her deck, and she wanted to play Truth or Dare. I said Truth, because I hate the kind of stuff you have to do if you get dared, like call up innocent people and say, We're conducting a sex survey, and would you mind telling us how many times a week you do it, and in what positions?

So, anyway, she said, Are you a virgin? I had to say no. No! she says, shrieking and falling over backwards in a pretend swoon, like that was the most outrageous thing she'd ever heard of in her life.

I said, Now it's your turn, and she goes, Truth! so I said, Are you? and she goes, *No, and I love it!*

And right then—it's hard to explain—I wanted to throttle her. Because Alex may be a little on the creepy side, but at least he's a boyfriend, and if she wanted to, she could have lots of boyfriends since she's really pretty.

And lately I can't stop remembering what my mom said, even though at the time she apologized and admitted she was being unfair. That with quote unquote *that* in me none of the boys my age were going to want to have anything to do with me. Or else they were going to get the wrong idea and be trying to get in my pants all the time.

I said some ugly things to her, too, but nothing as mean as that.

Because now I can't forget it. I couldn't forget it yesterday when I went skinny-dipping with my dad in the Wahaneeka Reservoir.

It was hot out. You're not supposed to mind your own bad smells, but I can tell you from experience, it's not true. Depending on which way the wind was blowing, I kept getting whiffs of unwashed armpit or worse.

I was making myself sick.

I did it once before, I went skinny-dipping in a stream, but that didn't count, because there weren't any other people around. If you do it by yourself, it's like you know what.

There were cars parked on the side of the road. We turned down a path. Back in there, the woods smelled like cucumbers, but I couldn't find any. Some of the leaves were beginning to turn yellow.

I had my doubts, since people would see how far I stuck out. But a part of me wanted to go where other people were, especially males, and if necessary, stare down their rude, impudent looks.

I wanted the whole world to see the naked truth once

and for all, and have to accept me as I am, not as they want me to be.

I wanted to strike up an acquaintance with a cute boy who would want to be my boyfriend in spite of my womb the size of a basketball and not make too many demands on me, but be there when I needed him. For moral support.

Plus, we could kiss a lot.

A reservoir is like a lake. Pretty soon you could hear people calling to each other and catch glimpses of pink bodies through the trees. My dad nudged me with his bony elbow, I guess because I was starting to take baby steps. Cut it out, I said. (I'm sorry, but he acts so goony sometimes.)

He was the one who thought it would be good for me—coming back out in Society. But I could tell he was also worried, knowing the attendant dangers.

Clothes were hanging on all the bushes. There were shoes under the branches.

It was hard to believe at first, but everybody really was naked—except for this Boy Scout troop out on patrol, standing in some bushes partway down the shore, pretending to be looking at the water. They could hardly believe their eyes, probably.

It was only people's bodies. Hadn't they ever seen anyone's body before?

Once we got to the water's edge, my dad, I'm embarrassed to say, started really getting into it, kicking his shoes off, unbuttoning his shirt.

I undid one shoelace.

He jerked his head to the side, which means, What's the matter, Bizzy?

Under my breath I said, This is sick.

But no one else was making that big a deal about it, and after a while it felt kind of queer to be the only one wearing clothes—like the time I went all dressed up to Samantha Malm's party and everyone else was wearing shorts, which happened in New Hampshire about three lifetimes ago.

Finally, I took a deep breath, closed my eyes, and took my shirt off, but nobody laughed or whistled or even looked.

My dad kept rotating his poor face in the sun like he was the main course at a barbecue or something.

I was afraid that if I didn't go in, mushrooms would start growing in my pits. So I peeled down my pants the rest of the way and took off my shoes and socks.

I'm not a nudist, but I have to admit I'm getting to like walking around naked outdoors.

We hobbled over to where we could see my reflection in the water—pink wiggles. He made me go first, backwards, feeling for footholds, while he stood guard, glancing over his shoulder. The w-water was f-freezing, but after about ten seconds you got used to it, and I could feel days of crud melting off.

Come on, I called, so my dad dove over me and came up spouting water like some kind of sea creature. Like the Loch Ness Monster.

Nobody paid that much attention except for this one hirsute woman who kept staring at me without smiling. There was also a guy sunning himself on a rock, who kept looking for chiggers or whatever under his balls.

My dad goes poke, poke, poke, which means, Race you to the other side, kiddo, and started churning away, before I even had a chance to agree. But I easily caught up and passed him and won. It wasn't that great a victory. I've taken swimming lessons since I was five and know how to breathe, whereas my dad tries to keep his head above water, like a dog, which slows you down. That's a mistake a lot of people make.

Anyway, we ended up on the other shore, sitting by ourselves in the shallow water where it was warm and muddy. The mud didn't look too appetizing and smelled a little like the fertilizer our next-door neighbor puts on his lawn, but I figured what's natural can't hurt you.

This was probably the last day of the year warm enough to swim, and everyone wanted to take advantage of it. Everywhere you looked, you saw bodies splashing in the water or climbing on the rocks. Strangely enough, it wasn't that sexy. I mean, at first it was, sort of, but after a while you just accepted it. The feelings got spread out in all of Nature, in the sounds you could hear distinctly from way across the lake or the dizzying smell of pine needles or the bobbing of the baby blue waves. You felt like you belonged, like you were a part of everything.

If you've never tried it, you should.

For a long time I just sloshed around, floating on my back, dragging my heels, like I was a little boat caught in the reeds, wondering what if anything Effie could feel, imagining her in her own little body of water, like a miniature me.

Then after a while I stood up and started washing my hair as best I could, using sand for soap. And then we started walking along in the shallow water, which was up to our knees.

I figured that when I stood up with my back straight and crossed my arms, I looked like any other teenager who had been on a cookie binge.

Up ahead two college boys were swinging by a thick

rope tied to a tree. They both smiled when I approached, and the cuter of the two asked me if I wanted to try. He was standing on the lowest branch and used a stick to snag the rope, which he held out to me. It looked sort of like a dead snake, the end all wet and sandy, and at first I didn't want to touch it.

I turned to my dad, who was shivering and hugging himself. He didn't say anything one way or the other. So I took the rope and climbed up the bank as high as I could, and then holding it over my head I started running and swung out over the water. My body turned sideways and my feet flew apart, but I could have cared less. Just before I hit the water the other guy said, Oh, oh, belly smacker. And he was right, but it didn't hurt that much. I came up laughing. Everyone was laughing except for my dad, who had moved back in the woods to blend in with the shadows, the way he always does when I'm feeling the least bit female.

Sometimes I get so tired of dragging him everywhere like an overgrown Raggedy Andy with his face rubbed off.

I scrambled up the bank. The rope swung back, and the boy in the tree caught it with his stick. My dad was hiding behind a rock with just his eyes peering out. I gave him one of my blue looks, walked to the top of the bank again, and pulled down on the rope like I was ringing a bell. This time I lifted my legs and waited until the last minute before letting go. Then I started flapping my arms like crazy, like I thought I was a bird or something and could just fly away. But instead, *whoosh*, the world disappeared, I sank deeper and deeper in the dark, green lake, came to a slow stop, rolled forward like a fetus. There was a thumping sound all around me like a heartbeat.

178

Part of me wanted to stay down there forever, turn into mud. Turn into an old snapping turtle, with moss growing on my back. Then if any ugly feet should descend into my kingdom, I'd paddle over and bite their toes. I even grabbed some weeds growing on the bottom, but they were too slimy to hold on to. Milling the water with my arms, I tried swallowing the whole lake like the fifth Chinese brother, but the air in my lungs had other plans. It lifted me up, up, up. I rose through the silver surface like a fat buoy.

My dad had come down to the edge of the lake. He was peering into the water, looking worried. Then the boy in the tree whizzed by overhead, shouting, Geronimo!

I was coughing and spitting. "Come on, you old Bone," I cried, the tears burning my wet face. And without waiting I started back, knowing full well he'd follow.

&
& &
&   &
&& &&

It's raining, but I can't go back to the house. We were foraging when it started. I thought I heard someone yell, Bizzy! but now all I hear is the rain coming down. My dad literally dove into the woods. I tried to dive, too, but ended up in a pricker bush.

I didn't see anyone. It sounded like people were running and shouting. There was lightning.

My heart got so big I thought it would catch on my ribs. I kept leaping over fallen branches, kicking up leaves and toadstools. I twisted my ankle for the second time, this time on a big root, but I can still walk.

I made it to the lean-to behind the house, where to be on the safe side I used to keep my food, when I had some. Then I squatted down and waited. It's pretty dry in here, except every once in a while the wind shakes the trees and I get a shower. It trickles down the back of my neck and makes the paper wrinkle.

Dad? I keep whispering. Dad, where are you?

Only hours to go now. I hope I make it.

I know it's only my imagination, but a minute ago I had this feeling my mom was watching me. I said, Mom? She stood over there, under the tree, her white dress aglow like foxfire. I could hear her breathing in the rain.

I came to say good-bye, she whispered.

Good-bye?

I put my hands in my armpits to keep them from freezing. I wriggle around in my nest like Big Bird, trying to get comfortable—but there's always something sticking in my back or my leg.

We're going to miss you, dear.

A wisp of hair hung down over her eyes. A will-o'-the-wisp. I tried to brush it away.

I stared at her until it started to rain hard and the rain blotted out everything. It also made a terrible racket. I had to shout what was on my mind. I'M SORRY FOR MESS-ING UP YOUR LIFE!

At the sound of my voice a little deer started up in the underbrush, not more than ten yards from where I'm sitting. I could practically have touched her! She thumped off somewhere.

Needless to say, I jumped about a mile. Then I started laughing. I laughed and laughed.

The rain droned on, incessant.

I had to write this much down. I would give anything for a cheeseburger. I'm wondering when it'll be safe to go back because it's getting too dark to see and I'm cold.

```
        &
     &     &
   &         &
 &             &
 Dear     Ef
 fie           &
 &&&&&&&
```

&

Dear Effie,

Your house is on a hill and has this really awesome view. From where I'm sitting, in an old rocking chair I lugged up from the basement, you can see for miles in every direction. Mrs. Trowbridge, the village idiot and a relative of ours (naturally), lives thataway, over the tops of the trees that are starting to turn yellow.

I always get slightly lost when I'm coming back from her house because you have to start out in the wrong direction, but it's the only way to get here (the road winds).

An old car is permanently parked in the sugar beet field. It hasn't budged since the beginning of history, probably, and the color of its paint job is somewhere between green and blue. It is not, however, a Chevrolet. I checked. Next to it is a farm implement with a giant lobster claw reaching out of the back, but it's a harmless monster, so don't be afraid. As a matter of fact, don't be afraid of anything.

This is your room, Effie. I'm going to bring you in here, all plump and pink and squirmy from your bath. And on the changing table you're going to arch your back and try to see over your head, like most of the babies I've baby-sat for do, while I desperately try to thread your pudgy arms through the holes of your cotton nightshirt.

Your crib is going to go along that wall. While you're sleeping, I'm going to work quietly, fixing the place up. I'm going to hang fresh paper with little flowers on it on the walls.

I'll rent a sanding machine and redo all the floors downstairs, so that when you wake up you can crawl wherever you want to without getting splinters in your chubby knees. In the kitchen and bathroom I'm going to tear up the buckled linoleum and put new tiles down.

I'll get a book from the library that tells you how.

A honking of Canada geese just flew overhead—you and I both jumped a mile. So now I get to make a wish (I make up my own rules about things like that). I *wwwiiissshhh* that someday, right in the middle of puking up your mushed-up ham and beans all over your granny's nice new dress, you will suddenly focus your thundercloud gray eyes on her chin and break out your snapping-turtle smile. The way babies do. And she won't be able to help it, she will fall in love with you the way she did with me. Amen.

(I wasn't exactly planned or entirely wanted, either.)

Please don't think because of some of the snide remarks you may have overheard through the warm and viscous walls of my womb that I don't love my mom. I do. She's the most important person in my life.

It's just that being her daughter isn't always easy. For one thing, she's a hard act to follow. I can sympathize with people like Princess Caroline or Caroline Kennedy, not that my mom's really famous, but given a different set of circumstances, I honestly believe she could have been anything she wanted. A Hollywood director. A politician. The first woman president if she wanted.

We've been through a hard time, as you know. But you want to hear something strange? We also haven't hugged each other so much since I was a little chimpanzee (like you). It's hard to explain—it's like there's this new bond between us, especially when we're discussing men and how immature they are and what a weenie Barry Comstock is. Then it's like we're like sisters-at-arms.

The one point I'm afraid we're always going to disagree on is S. Leicester (Les) Smith. I know you've never taken a psych course, either, but doesn't it seem obvious to you that the reason she's like the inside of a roasted marshmallow after you've pulled the black part off where he's concerned is that having been burned one way or another by her first four husbands, she desperately wants to marry someone *safe*, even if it means going against her own true beliefs and feelings?

Hattie Topham Brooke, etc., wants to marry someone who will (1) never go to war and get killed, (2) never get caught with a bomb in his briefcase, skip bail, and run away to Canada, (3) never turn out not to be a Hungarian count with a second family on the other side of the Iron Curtain, (4) never try to cross that invisible line between what's good healthy affection between stepfather and stepdaughter, and what's taboo (thank you, Jesus, thank you, Lord, S. Leicester doesn't have the imagination to do anything bad, for which we can all be eternally grateful).

I really would like for you to have a nice grandfather, but in my opinion no grandfather is better than a person who, when you go to talk to him, starts smiling at you with the corners of his mouth—or at least that's what you think he's doing—so you get your hopes up and smile back. But then his smile vanishes, you realize it's just a nervous tic or something, and there you are, looking like one of those Have-a-nice-day faces Ms. Plover always used to draw at the bottom of my papers.

Because his eyes *never* smile.

I honestly think sometimes that Les is my ultimate punishment for what I did last spring with my previous stepfather. Mom said once that she hoped he would have a good influence on me, make me more courteous and cheerful. I should have done my Brer Rabbit routine: Pulease, Mom, I can't get enough of men who think of life as a football game. If you marry him, we could all be part of a winning team.

Then probably to spite me she would have said, Sorry, Biz, but the wedding's off.

& &

It was August 30, the day before I packed my clothes and fled. We were down in the basement of Leicester Smith's house in northern Virginia, sorting clothes. I hasten to add that I'm not any man's slave, and neither is my mom, but for some reason she seemed to think we should act like guests in his house, at least until the wedding, after which we'll be able to afford to hire what she jokingly calls a *wife*—i.e., a Vietnamese woman who isn't that interested in making documentary videos.

Les was kind enough to take us in, quote unquote, and we wanted to show our gratitude in every way we could.

I admit I was in an ornery mood—not because of the housework per se, since somebody had to do it and he changed the oil in her car and did other things that made it run right for the first time in years.

But because all S. (Standish?) L. Smith's socks were navy blue.

What does it tell you about a person that he has a two-week supply of calf-length navy blue socks, all of them exactly the same, so that all you do to sort them is lay them together two by two, roll them into a knot, and fire them with all your might into the plastic basket in the corner?

Mom didn't say, Uh, Biz, cut it out already with the socks, because she was too busy trying to explain that Les might not be a warm person—which she knew was what mattered to young people like me—but that he *meant well.* And if that wasn't enough to make a potential step-daughter bow down and kiss the toes of his navy blue socks, *he also wanted to be friends* with me. It was just that he found my sense of humor a little hard to take. He could never tell if I was just trying to be funny or if I was being impudent and mocking him.

I should probably mention that Standish's ancestors came over on the *Mayflower* seventeen generations ago, a fact that he quite frequently lets slip into the conversation

189

and which probably has a lot to do with how serious he is all the time, especially about real estate and why it's smart to leave the People's Republic of Taxachusetts, where he was born and where it costs I can't remember how much a year to heat your house in the winter, and the taxes are outrageously high compared to those in a warmer and more convenient state like northern Virginia.

I borrowed his calculator. A person has two parents and four grandparents and eight great-grandparents, right?

All 131,072 of them? I asked. It's amazing the *Mayflower* ever landed, ha ha.

I don't know whether he got it or not, but he looked at me with infinite sadness, like he thought I was definitely going to hell for being sacrilegious all the time. Like there was nothing he or anyone else could do to save me, except maybe tithe and pray.

Mom does agree that he gives in too readily to his daughter Kate's demands, but she says it's because they've had a difficult life.

(Mom can forgive anyone anything, as long as they've "had a difficult life," unless, of course, it's someone she doesn't like anymore, like one of her sexually immature former husbands. Her ancestors must have come over on a missionary boat or something.)

I don't mean to be lacking in Gratitude. Les's house really is convenient. It has central air, which costs I can't remember how much a year to fuel in the summer and, therefore, you don't have to waste time opening the windows and letting in the smell of grass being mowed or the sounds of birds chirping. It has wall-to-wall carpeting so you can give all your mops away to the poor, thereby reducing taxes—though, to tell you the truth, under the fresh pine scent in the downstairs bathroom there's a slight pissy smell. It has cable, so you can watch smut anytime you want to, which Kate sneaks downstairs all the time to do.

Plus—more good news—the Fairfax County school system is either the *best,* or *one of the best,* in the country, I can't remember which. In another year, if I learned all the words in this book she bought me, *How to Increase Your Vocabulary and Win at the SATs,* I could go to the college of my choice. You name it, she said, Harvard, Yale, Princeton. Brown is supposed to be up there, too. Dartmouth, if I really had my heart set on going back to New Hampshire. Penn as a backup. Most of the people she knew would be overjoyed if their children had my Gifts and Abilities.

I learned the first word, *abjure:* a verb, to renounce, foreswear, or disavow—but I'm hopeless when it comes to learning things from lists, and unfortunately I left the book on a park bench somewhere, which means I'll probably flunk the SATs and end up going to a community college, along with all the other unwed mothers.

For about the millionth time she reminded me of what my English teacher at Steerforth had said about my "love of literature" and my "way with words." She agreed Ms. Plover was a gnat brain, but said at least she was right about that.

Yes, she said, Michigan was a good school, too. Not as good. We could talk about that when the time came.

Yes, she said, she remembered that when we were marrying Barry Comstock she'd said she was doing it partly so that I could go to Steerforth Academy as a faculty child and get this excellent education there for free.

Are you intentionally trying to humiliate me? she asked.

After a brief silence, during which it dawned on her that my red sweatshirt had run all over one of Les's white shirts, making it—egad!—pink, she added almost absent-mindedly that she knew without my telling her that she wasn't perfect. And that more than anything she wanted to save me from making some of the mistakes she had made.

I said, I learn by going where I have to go.

That's from a poem we read last year in school. I can't tell you the author's name because I don't remember. But always quote famous writers when you're having an argument with your parents, because they never can think of anything to say back.

I said, Whoso would be a person must be a noncon-formist.

Perhaps I hear a different drummer, I said.

Truce? she said. I remember, I was cutting up vegetables to go in the salad. So I looked at her and smiled. *What was it like when you were pregnant?*

She was making my all-time favorite dinner, chicken oregano. Mom may not be all that good at sweeping and mopping, but she's an awesome cook, especially when it comes to chicken oregano, my favorite.

You take a chicken and rub it all over with olive oil and chopped-up garlic, and then while that's getting started in the oven, you cut your potatoes up into bite-size pieces and pour the rest of the olive oil and garlic over them, plus lemon juice and salt and pepper and oregano, using your hands to make sure everything is good and gooey. Then you dump the whole thing in the pan with the chicken about the time it starts turning sunset brown. And in about an hour, if you can survive that long, it's steaming up from under your knife and fork.

Chicken oregano is better than sex, in my opinion.

What exactly do you want to know? she said, and I said, Everything, like how you first found out.

Well, she said, rubbing oregano between the palms of her big hands, in those days they didn't have kits you could just buy in the drugstore and do at home. In the privacy of your own bathroom. You had to pee in a jelly jar and take it to the doctor's so that everybody knew, or you felt that they did. And then they performed what was called the rabbit test, where they took some of your pee and injected it into a virgin rabbit. And, if I remember right, its little ovaries were supposed to turn red and swell all up if the test was positive.

I bet the rabbit didn't like that very much, I said. Then I stopped with the peeler in midair and said, Oh, gross, you mean they had to kill it first?

She made her does-this-mean-I-have-to-be-the-one-to-tell-you-where-babies-come-from? face.

That's terrible, I said, putting down the peeler. I starting slicing the carrot as thinly as I could because Kate, my supposedly future stepsister, will only eat carrots in salads if they're very thinly sliced, and this was one of my ways of showing Gratitude.

I know, she said. I felt awful. I felt jinxed, almost.

So why didn't you get an abortion?

(Because nowadays to hear her talk you'd think every woman should get pregnant as fast as she can so that afterwards she can get rid of the fetus, thereby making the correct political statement. Like if Mom had to do it over again, she'd have me up the vacuum tube before you can say *Our Bodies, Ourselves!*)

She started out by saying, Well, to tell you the truth, it was much more of a hassle in those days. She didn't have anyone to talk to. Her mother would have been horrified. She couldn't even tell her mom she was pregnant until after "Ricky" and she were engaged. Her dad was more with it, but they never talked about things like that. We hardly ever talked about anything important, except for politics, she said, which always led to violent fights. All she could think of was how expensive it would be. And scary.

I had visions, she said, of going to a back room somewhere in downtown Detroit, of a seedy-looking doctor with a coat hanger behind his back. Those were the stories you heard.

But then she couldn't resist the opportunity of bringing up the Population Explosion for the umpteenth time. In the time it takes you to blow your nose or flush the toilet, I can't remember which, thousands of new babies are born, especially in places like India and Brazil. And the statistics on teenage pregnancy are enough to give you a stroke. I'm not good at numbers, but it's something like in every third booth at the Burger King there's at least one pregnant teenager.

And the result of all this, besides the obvious fact that all these babies are to blame for the overdevelopment of our precious parklands, is that the competition for getting into the nation's best schools has become *unimaginable*. It's like if you think of a cheering crowd at a high-school basketball game all applying to Harvard, Princeton, and Yale, less than one person there, percentage-wise—say just a head and torso minus the genitals—would be admitted. The stands might as well collapse under the rest of them because, without a quality education, how were they ever going to get ahead in life?

My problem was that I didn't know how lucky I was to live in a time when a woman could choose, so that she didn't have to think of every pregnancy as an automatic life sentence—blah, blah, blah.

I didn't say anything, but I was tempted to pick up the salad bowl, like it was a Frisbee or something, and calmly sail it across the kitchen into the breakfast nook. Where it would of course shatter the glass in the little lattice windows and send sliced radishes and cucumbers out into the flower beds behind the house.

And she would go, Why, Biz, what's the matter?

But, instead, I quietly put some of the salad in a separate dish, since Kate will only eat it plain. It was against my better judgment, but another token of my Gratitude. I poured oil on the rest of the salad and started tossing lightly.

Slow and easy, like I was just trying to make conversation, I said, *Weren't you ever glad to be pregnant?*

I was confused, Mom said. I knew I wanted to have kids eventually. A part of me was thrilled. I remember standing in front of the mirror with my nightgown bunched up in front of me, doing pirouettes, whispering, I'm going to be a mother!

&
&&&

Nothing had happened yet to make me want to get the hell out of there. It was just a day like any of the 169 others before it, August 30, P.E. (i.e., Post Effie). After supper we went to Tyson's Corner to try on clothes, and within ten minutes I had found what I was looking for, a yellow sundress, which I could start wearing right away and sort of expand in as my tummy grew.

Mom, however, kept plugging this pale blue back-to-school outfit that was made out of seersucker and would have been very nice under any other circumstances, being exactly the kind of outfit moms always want to buy their daughters—only at the time it just barely fit me around the waist, and there was no way to let it out without spoiling the style.

I could feel its death grip on my womb, so, needless to say, I started giving everybody in the Varsity Shop my blue look. Especially the saleslady, who was probably just an innocent bystander, only she made the mistake of agreeing with everything my mom said and adding some little gems of her own like, Oh, honey, the boys aren't going to be able to stand it when they see you coming in this number!

Mom must have finally recognized the danger signs, like when I asked the saleslady if she believed in a supreme being and the sanctity of human life. Mom put her hand on the back of her neck and started giving herself a massage, which she always does when she's stressed out and trying to relax.

We'll take the sundress, she said to the saleslady in her most gracious voice—lately it even has a touch of Southern accent in it. We'll have to think about the other one.

So that isn't what made me leave. Because instead of having one of our usual fights, we went to the Olde Dominion Ice Cream Parlour for a hot-fudge cream-puff sundae, and almost immediately we both started feeling sisterly again. Or at least I did. It helped that she agreed the saleslady looked exactly like a dachshund that somebody had taught to dance on its hind legs.

And while I was carefully portioning my sundae so that every bite contained the exact same amount of cream puff, ice cream, and hot fudge, right to the last luxurious lick, I said, *What kinds of things did you use to fight about?*

Meaning her and my dad, because lately she likes to go around saying that their marriage never would have lasted, probably, due to the difference in their backgrounds and the fact that they fought all the time.

Everything, she said. Your father wasn't a saint that you should sacrifice your life to immortalize him, you know.

What is that supposed to mean?

He could be pigheaded and grumpy. He was a terrible chauvinist—always saying a mother should stay home and take care of her kids. He had a temper.

Then because I was starting to flash blue, she quickly added, With children and animals he was always very gentle.

She said, Our biggest fights were about the Vietnam War, which I was dead set against. I'm not trying to sound superior or anything—it's just that I had finished half of my junior year in college and attended some of the teach-ins at the University of Michigan. I had seen some very upsetting photographs that would have changed anybody's mind. I gave him the novel *Catch-22* in the hopes that it would open his eyes to the futility of war.

Instead it made him all the more determined to go. All he could think of was how neat it would be to fly jets and have lots of buddies to gripe with. And whenever I tried to tell him about what our soldiers were really doing over there, to innocent peasants, he would get this look in his eyes that said, You may be smarter than me and read the paper more, but I don't believe you, and if you keep saying stuff like that, I may start hating you.

She said, You saw that look a lot in the 60s.

I licked the last smudge of hot fudge off my spoon and wondered, eyeing the other customers, if any of them would seriously object to my cleaning my dish the same way.

When he got his draft notice, she said, I tried to talk him into running away with me to Canada. I knew some people in Montreal. You never saw anyone more indignant in your life. What do you think I am, he said, a coward?

She-it, no! I said, imitating my dad's Michigan accent, which she taught me to do a long time ago. She looked over at me and, almost like she hadn't meant to, broke into a grin.

&
& &
& &

All that was very chummy. We drove home, having bought the sundress for me, tights for Kate (Mom's gift), and socks for Les (my gift—maroon ones, ankle length). Plus some groceries we stopped at Kroger's to get.

I remember, I was looking out the window at all the cars, the ones with headlights going one way, the ones with taillights going the other. Each one a story unto itself, but when you're on the road they just seem like the river of life or whatever.

Tell me how you found out he was dead.

I should mention that I'm forever asking about stuff like that. I know all the stories by heart but never get tired of hearing them. I pity kids who have to grow up on "The Brady Bunch" and "Family Ties." I mean, if that's where they get their ideas about families from.

Me, I grew up on stories about my dad, and how he and my mom met when she dropped out of college like everybody else in the 60s and came up to this house—supposedly to do a photographic exposé of the poor migrant cherry pickers, but really just to be a flower child and hang out. And then because she and Ricky were too horny to use birth control or whatever—not the sort of thing I ever asked about—she got pregnant, and her world changed forever.

199

Mom's pretty frank about her love life and other things I'm not sure I'm going to want to tell you when you're young. Whether that's been good for me or not, only the headshrinkers can say—the rest of us haven't studied the subject enough in college. Personally I'm not sorry, since these stories are my family myths and legends. When I was younger, if she tried to change even the smallest detail, I'd get all indignant, the way little children do, and say, That's not right! That's not how it happened!

Sometimes, if I'm lucky, she'll add a detail—a new piece of information, not something that contradicts my picture, but instead fills it in.

And then I see my dad a little more clearly, with his nose slightly tilted, which gives him a semimocking look, sort of like James Dean—who she really did say he looked like once when we were watching *East of Eden* on the VCR, though she denies it now out of her fear that I'll make him into some kind of superhero. From what I infer, their love life must have been pretty awesome.

What do you want to know that you don't know already? she said, without turning to look at me. She always drives like that, with both hands on the steering wheel, her eyes glued to the road ahead. She looks vulnerable when she drives. Despite all the Jane Fonda exercises she does in front of the VCR and all the Oil of Olay she puts on her face, you can tell she isn't twenty-two anymore. I don't mind her pudgies in the middle or the wrinkles on her face from an aesthetic point of view, the way she does. But they do sort of make me feel uneasy.

You want to know the truth? They make me feel that the day is coming when there's not going to be anyone between me and the Hereafter. Like *I'm* going to have to be the older generation and pretend to know what's right and wrong when my teenage daughter comes to me and says, Guess what, Mom.

Yuk. I don't even want to think about that now.

So, anyway, she started telling me what for me is the greatest story ever told. How at first she was afraid her family would think the father of her child was a juvenile delinquent because of the way he combed his hair back. But instead they were *crazy* about him. Grandma thought he was quote unquote adorable, and Uncle Jimmy kept coming into the living room and saying things like, I just ran seven miles, think I'll go down in the basement and lift two hundred pounds. And how after their wedding and their pathetic honeymoon—because he only had two days' leave—he had to rush back to the army. They shipped him overseas, and Mom came up here. To sit in this very rocking chair, maybe, and look out the window, like I keep doing. And, using psychedelic yarn, to knit him and me matching sweaters, which I still have somewhere to this day.

Grandma and Grandpa came up to be with her on weekends, and when she got close to her due date, Grandma stayed.

Mom told me how they watched the news on television, and how the President kept saying everything would be all right, but she knew better than to believe him. For a while she tried to hate the Vietnamese, but how can you? she said. They went around in straw hats and what looked like pajamas, and half the time they smiled shyly at the camera, even if they were supposedly the enemy. And it wasn't our country, so what were we doing there, anyway?

My dad wrote that he was in the hospital—not with wounds, but with malaria! Now they'll have to send him home, said Grandma Topham, who always tries to look on the bright side.

For a long time they didn't hear anything. It was getting to be fall then, too. She had gone to lie down on the couch because she didn't feel so hot. Grandma called upstairs to say a letter had come. It was from somebody high up in Washington. The envelope was very light, which as anyone who has friends who've applied to Harvard, Princeton, or Yale knows, is bad news.

I only read it once. It gave me the creeps. It sounded so definite, like it had been written by God or something. Mom was crying. Grandma said, Darling, there's a letter from him, too. It came in the same mail. Do you feel like reading it now?

This is the letter I lost, though of course I know it by heart.

Hello Hattie,

I'm sorry I haven't written. I'm okay, so you don't have to worry. We're not suppose [*sic*] to say exactly where we are (Army regulations), but I'll tell you this much, I'm sitting in a tree (honest!). Every time I see something moving down on the road below, even if it's only a peasant or a kid on a bike, I have to report it, since we can't take any chances.

It's the middle of the night, but as long as I'm writing to you, I figure I'm still alive, though I may just be dreaming, ha ha. There's some kind of activity going on Northeast of here, because every few seconds there's a flash of light followed by what sounds like thunder, but it isn't thunder, it's the fighting. Well, enough about yours truly. I see that in spite of all your marches, etc., you haven't stopped the war yet (smile). Some of what you say makes sense, though. I hope you're taking good care of Sweetpea? I think of your boobs whenever I want to think of something happy.

This guy I know who got a pass and went back to the States supposedly made it seventeen times in one weekend with his girlfriend, but that's nothing, right Hattie?

Your husband,
Richard H. Brooke, Pfc.

Mom stayed here until after Thanksgiving, when the unaborted fetus, despite the fact that it had been conceived out of wedlock, to people who didn't have all that much in common, except for S-E-X, emerged with her head intact and exactly the right number of fingers and toes.

As soon as we pulled into the driveway of Les Smith's house, behind his Japanese car (which, of course, matches the color of his socks), and Mom turned off the engine, the crickets started chirping, like so many impatient little telephones ringing. Instead of getting right out, she turned to me and said, almost in an angry voice, *I have regrets, too.* As any single mother does. You will, too—don't kid yourself.

Then, because I was opening the door on my side: Look at me, Bizzy. I'm a remarkable woman—and that's not boasting, it's just stating a fact. I've put together a company that's made a name for itself. Two of my documentaries have been nominated for awards. I'm proud of that.

But I'm nothing like as successful as I could have been.

When I started out, I dreamed of making real movies, the kind you see in the theater. I wanted to make a movie about your dad in Vietnam. I even wrote a script.

Why don't you? I wanted to say. It wasn't too late. She could fly to Vietnam, hire a boat, and sail up the Mekong River. Who knows what she'd find. I mean, maybe a tall MIA, his face in shadow, really would slowly hobble over to the edge of the river, a brood of Amerasian kids hanging from his arm. At first they wouldn't even recognize each other, but then something about the way his ears stuck out, etc., etc.

But something told me to keep my trap shut.

If I hadn't had to finish school in the evening, she said, practically hissing. If I hadn't had to depend on other people's kindness to survive with a small child. If I hadn't had to put my career together in bits and pieces.

Then she started giving herself a neck rub.

I'm not complaining, she said. I made my decision for whatever overwhelming reasons, and I've lived with it. But I'll be goddamned if I'm going to sit back and watch you mess your life up and not say anything.

(Block your little shell-like ears, Effie. I'm sorry to say my mom always takes the Lord's name in vain, when she thinks you're not paying enough attention. And it's true, I was starting to see movies of my dad, in Vietnam, coming back to life.)

You have so much promise, Bizzy, she said. First, we're going to see you get the education you deserve—the head start I never had. Then, I promise that with your looks you're not going to have any trouble finding the right sort of man. You're too much for most high school boys, but just wait till you get to college, dot dot dot. You're going to find someone who will value you as an equal partner and want to share in the raising of your children so you really can make movies if you want to. Or write books. And I'm going to be so proud of you, precious!

I don't doubt for a minute you will have children eventually. But on your terms, when the time is right.

Speech apparently over, we carried in the packages, including a six-pack of Amstel Light for Les. I was headed upstairs to bed, when she called out after me:

Bizzy! (Yes, Mom.) When I was about your age, I read a biography of Michelangelo by Irving Stone. Oh, I realize now it was a very corny book, but it changed my life. It said that Michelangelo's great ambition, even when he was a small boy in the hills of Tuscany, was to *make something*. And I realized right then and there that that's what I wanted to do. I still do.

Then in a low, almost threatening voice, she said, looking up at me, You can do that, Biz. You have spunk. You're not afraid of going against stereotypes and what other people think of you. Even if it's hard. *You can make something.*

It was around midnight and I was sleeping the sleep of the innocent, when I felt something seize me by my heel. At first I thought it was the alligator Kate claims to have seen in the stream behind the house. I know there are no alligators back there—Kate's always saying stuff like that to get attention—but I did a somersault and landed on my pillow with my feet tucked firmly under me. After a couple of unsuccessful tries, I finally found the little lamp chain and turned on the light.

It was Mom in her nightgown like Lady Macbeth, pacing back and forth. She couldn't come right out and say, Please, Bizzy, please don't have the baby.

In a low voice she said, I think I'm going crazy.

I didn't say anything back. I only hugged my legs and rested my chin on my knees and stared at her. But the next morning I took off.

&
&&&
&&&

On September 14, as soon as the rates had changed, I walked to the gas station to call home collect. I had already rehearsed about a thousand times what I was going to say: Six months are up, it's against the law to get an abortion, so I can't abjure, but I'll do anything you want—load the dishwasher for a whole year, stop saying French is a fag language, apply to Harvard, etc.—but there was a recording on her answering machine, and all I could hear before the operator switched me off was, "Bizzy, I love you!"

Naturally I felt a little funny standing there in the truck fumes.

Then I tried to call Kate on the children's line her father had installed for her, but it was busy for at least half an hour. So I walked around hoping to find some money on the ground, and when I came back, the operator said, I'm busy, too, honey, and the phone was already ringing, so I shouted, My name is Elizabeth Anne Brooke, for crying out loud! and then Kate answered, and when the operator, somewhat chastened, said, Will you pay for the call? she hesitated for a second or two before saying she guessed so. And then right away she started saying stuff like, Boy, are you in trouble. Thanks to you, my dad isn't going to marry your mom anymore, and we can't call out on the other phone, because it has a message for you, so my dad has to use mine all the time, which sucks, and are you really pregnant? What's it like? And, Can I come there? It's so boring here, I hate it.

Then I walked back to the house and thought, What the heck, and used the big black phone downstairs to call Father Jude. To see if he would intercede between my mom and me, which he said he'd be glad to do. And you know something, Effie? He said he really believed my name was Iphigenia, which in a way is sweet, I guess, because it means he trusted me, so naturally at the time I couldn't help crying for all the lies I told, but you have to admit it would be pretty kabadocuckoo for a mother to really name her kid Iphigenia, considering what happened to her in mythology.

My name is Elizabeth Anne Brooke—get it, Bridges, Brooke? Bizzy is what everyone calls me. I wrote Iphigenia on the form where it said, What's your name? because it was all I could think of. And, to tell you the truth, half the time I think of both of us as Iphigenias—whatever that says about me. But don't worry, if you really do turn out to be a girl, I'm going to name you Mary Claire, after my mom's however-many-greats grandmother who came out here with her family in the 1800s when she was a child. And if you're a boy, your name will of course be Richard.

It's starting to get dark out. The tippy tops of the trees are turning red. Way in the distance I can see a man or boy in a red hunting hat pounding or chopping something. The noise comes all this way in disconnected *boinks*, like in a poorly synchronized movie. Or like the light from the stars, which has to travel for hundreds of years before it reaches you. There's a bonfire, too. I can't see the flames, but the smoke goes straight up for miles.

A pickup truck is driving along the farthest road, stopping to let someone out. She is saying thank you, adjusting her backpack, rubbing the back of her neck. And now she is looking around to get her bearings and starting to walk this way, across the fields. I'm going to go down and meet her.

MORSE HAMILTON was born in Michigan and has lived in Tennessee, Idaho, New York, Illinois, New Hampshire, Texas, Virginia, and Massachusetts. Besides being a writer, he is a father, husband, and teacher. He currently lives just outside Boston and teaches at Tufts University.